Gayle Kennedy is a member of the Wongaiibon Clan of NSW and was the Indigenous Issues editor and writer for *Streetwize Comics* from 1995–1998. In 2005 her poetry manuscript 'Koori Girl Goes Shoppin'' was shortlisted for the David Unaipon Award, and in 2006 she won the David Unaipon Award for *Me, Antman & Fleabag*, which was shortlisted for a Victorian Premier's Literary Award, a Deadly Award and commended in the Kate Challis RAKA Award. Gayle has published eleven children's books as part of the *Yarning Strong* (OUP) series, and six of these were nominated for the 2011 Deadly Award for Achievement in Literature.

Gayle runs writing workshops and has presented at writers festivals, schools and NAIDOC events, and has spoken nationally and internationally on her experience with disability. She was commissioned by Red Room Poetry to write a poem for the Carved Trees Exhibition at the State Library of NSW.

First Nations Classics

ME, ANTMAN & FLEABAG

GAYLE KENNEDY

UQP

First published 2007 by University of Queensland Press
PO Box 6042, St Lucia, Queensland 4067 Australia
Reprinted 2017
This First Nations Classics edition published 2024

University of Queensland Press (UQP) acknowledges the Traditional Owners and their custodianship of the lands on which UQP operates. We pay our respects to their Ancestors and their descendants, who continue cultural and spiritual connections to Country. We recognise their valuable contributions to Australian and global society.

uqp.com.au
reception@uqp.com.au

Cover design by Jenna Lee
Author photograph by Juno Gemes
Typeset in 11.5/16 pt Bembo Std by Post Pre-press Group, Brisbane
Printed in Australia by McPherson's Printing Group

Australian Government | Creative Australia

First Nations Classics are assisted by the Australian Government through Creative Australia, its principal arts investment and advisory body.

This project is supported by the Copyright Agency's Cultural Fund.

COPYRIGHTAGENCY CULTURAL FUND

A catalogue record for this book is available from the National Library of Australia.

ISBN 978 0 7022 6856 4 (pbk)
ISBN 978 0 7022 6992 9 (epdf)
ISBN 978 0 7022 6993 6 (epub)

University of Queensland Press uses papers that are natural, renewable and recyclable products made from wood grown in well-managed forests and other controlled sources. The logging and manufacturing processes conform to the environmental regulations of the country of origin.

FSC www.fsc.org MIX Paper | Supporting responsible forestry FSC® C001695

For my brother Clem 'Buddy' Kennedy
I still miss you

Contents

Introduction
by Jared Thomas

I'm absolutely delighted to introduce the First Nations Classics edition of Gayle Kennedy's *Me, Antman & Fleabag*. It's my all-time favourite work of fiction by an Aboriginal author, an incredibly authentic story, and one that is deserving of so much attention. There are few works by Aboriginal authors that contain such balance between outrageously funny black humour and poignant depiction of explicit racism towards Aboriginal people and communities, as well as the indignities we sometimes endure at the hands of well-intentioned people. Most importantly, the effects of prejudice and racism are articulated by Kennedy, evoking a deep visceral response in the reader, one that personally fills my heart with pride in Kennedy as a storyteller, and my people for their strength and resilience.

In a former life as a lecturer, I loved introducing Australian film and literature students to *Me, Antman & Fleabag*. As a class we'd read at least the first two chapters aloud and students would be in tears with laughter when reading 'How ta drink in the park' and 'When Ronnie met Myrtle'. In addition to providing exceptional comedy, these two stories present the reader two very important truths about Aboriginal Australia: that we're often penalised for doing things that non-Indigenous Australians take for granted, such as drinking in public; and secondly, we're big-hearted and kind people. The establishment of these ideas early in the work is important because we're then introduced to a raft of characters who are big drinkers and dope smokers, and the humanity of the characters can shine beyond the stigma associated with these behaviours.

Part of the novel's charm is that it takes on a different format to a regular novel. Some of the chapters, for example, are no more than several paragraphs long, and each chapter could be deemed as a standalone short story except for the fact that there's always an inclusion of the central protagonists. Each story adds to the narrative arc of these key characters, helping us to understand the love 'Me, Antman and Fleabag' have for each other, and the reckoning of their experiences as Aboriginal people.

The novel weaves together elements of experience that are true for many Aboriginal people, such as becoming disconnected from family and Country, and also reconnecting to family and Country, the sense of loss and isolation because of colonisation, and the importance of friendships and humour to assist healing.

While characters are described in much detail upon introduction, such as Old Mother Howard ('She's got hair that's flat and greasy and the same colour as that grey shit ya git outta blocked up drains.'), a sense of mystery is maintained around Antman. This mystery around Antman helps to propel the novel and heightens our understanding of the beautiful bond between the central characters as the book concludes.

Gayle Kennedy is a member of the Wongaibon Clan of the Ngiyampaa-speaking Nation of south-west New South Wales. Gayle currently lives in Sydney and is a fan of country music. The blending of country music, particularly Slim Dusty's, is one of the very beautiful elements that shines through. The stories contained within her novel often resemble great country songs and campfire yarns, and I see the stories as ones that will be loved particularly by Aboriginal families into the future.

Two of the most difficult stories in the novel include 'The golden wedding anniversary' and 'Me, Antman and Fleabag hook up'. 'The golden wedding anniversary' deals with the issue of sexual assault of Aboriginal women by white men, something that many Aboriginal families have had to reckon with and, in this story, the characters Uncle Vic and Aunty Bess offer a recommendation for ways to forgive and an example is set through their relationship.

While not specifically a Stolen Generations story, the chapter 'Me, Antman and Fleabag hook up' speaks to the difficulty of disconnection from family and what it means for Aboriginal people to operate within a context where their Aboriginality is apparent to others, but they haven't fully found a way to reconnect with their family and deal with feelings of isolation.

It is the comedy that is wrapped around and between these types of stories within the novel that makes them very accessible to both an Aboriginal and non-Indigenous audience, providing a framework for healing and change.

Kennedy is a self-confessed rambler, so it's easy to assume, especially given the power of the voices of the characters, that her work is autobiographical, but, for the most part, the novel is fictional. The two aspects of Kennedy's own life that enter the narrative are those of family stories shared with her about the hardships her family and other Aboriginal families endured when Aboriginal men fought in World War Two, and Gayle's experience of being hospitalised as a child with polio. This knowledge helps us to understand the incredible tenderness with which this story is written.

Me, Antman & Fleabag was first published in 2007 at the time that National Indigenous Television was established, opening pathways for emerging Aboriginal directors and producers. It is my hope that the Aboriginal producers and directors of today see the great potential of *Me, Antman & Fleabag* for adaptation to the screen as either a feature film or a television series, particularly while Kennedy has the desire and energy to contribute to what will be an incredibly unique, important and enjoyable experience for audiences.

Gayle Kennedy's *Me, Antman & Fleabag* is an important addition to UQP's First Nations Classics series, and I am pleased to know that through this edition, a new generation of audiences will have the opportunity to engage with this delightful work.

How ta drink in the park

Me, Antman and our mongrel, Fleabag, like partyin outside. We both come from the bush. Me, I'm a NSW desert girl and Antman's mob are river people. Cos we aint got no river or desert here in the city, we like sittin in the park yarnin, havin a charge, playin country music. We don't cause no harm. Try tellin that to the coppers. Soon as they see us they start growlin. They say, 'No drinkin here', 'No music' and 'Git that dog registered'. Stuff like that. Then ya git sick of it and stay home and party in a yard the size of an old hanky with trains roarin by every time ya favourite song comes on.

We whinged bout it one day to Antman's cuz, Damien. He's a lawyer. Travelled round the world. He reckons we go about things the wrong way. Reckons we give up too easy. Says whitefullas aint the enemy. Says they love drinkin and partyin outside too. He says they got it worked out so coppers don't bother em. He showed us.

First he shouts Fleabag twelve months rego and a new collar in the Koori colours. Too deadly! Then he says the dog has to have a bath. Gawd Fleabag bunged on. Had to drag him out from under the house. He carried on like we was murderin him. Wouldn't come near us for hours after. His guts got the better of him though and he come in for a feed. He got over it. Smelt good too.

Then we got an esky and a couple of fancy bottles of wine. Damien reckons no casks or flagons. Besides, the bottles got twist tops now, so once ya finished, ya fill em up with cheap stuff for next time. We pack a nice blanket and a picnic. Nothin fancy; bread, cold meat, tomatoes, a big old lamb bone for Fleabag. We pile in Damien's car and head to Balmain. Damien lives there.

We pull up at this deadly park right on the harbour. Antman and me are a bit nervous, but Fleabag's outta the car and beltin cross the grass like there's no tomorrow. There's heaps of other dogs there, but that's okay cos he got his nuts cut out a couple a years ago so he don't go bluin no more.

We git the stuff outta the car, spread the blanket with the tucker, glasses and wine on the grass and sit down, still nervous. Then we see all these whitefullas. They're all sittin round with wine, beer and tucker too! They're havin a laugh. Kids and dogs are runnin round. There's no trains, the harbour's shinin, boats everywhere. We pour drinks; make sandwiches. People smile at us. They pat old Flea and fuss over his fancy collar. He laps it up.

And there's no coppers in sight!

Antman grins. 'Makes ya wanna sing, aye tidda?'

'Sure does,' I say, and whack old Slim in the CD player.

We know the drill and go every week now. Flea's used to havin a tub too. Knows he's goin to the park afterwards. Anyway, when we git sick of city life we go out bush, sometimes to visit my mob or sometimes Antman's. Ant's a builder so he goes whenever one job finishes. I do bar work or waitressin so I aint tied down either. Fleabag just comes along for the ride.

When Ronnie met Myrtle

Uncle Ronnie Harris and his dog, Flash, are big meat eaters. Their favourite is mutton. Uncle Ronnie likes to go out and get his own sheep from one of the local properties and kill it and hang it himself. He don't like meat from butcher shops. Reckons it's got a real 'chemically' smell and taste.

He cooks mutton every which way ya can, but his favourite way to do it is in a camp oven, in the coals, with camp oven vegetables and great heap of damper cooked in the ashes with lots of butter drippin off it. Whenever anyone comes back home from other places they been livin, he uses that as an excuse to bung on a camp oven do and invites everyone around. Reckons ya aint home till ya had a decent feed a slow-cooked mutton and beer, nice and chilled in an esky and a few hours of listenin to ya own mob tellin tall tales and singin along to Slim Dusty. Slim Dusty's real big out our way. All the blackfullas love Slim. We love stories and all Slim's songs tell a story. Besides, him and his family used ta bring their travellin country show out to the back country all the time. We all got memories of him and his family singin in our old hall, signin autographs, posin for photos.

Anyway, one time after me, Antman and Fleabag come home to chill out and mingle with the mob, Uncle Ronnie, happy as a pig in shit, comes round and tells us ta drop by on the weekend with a coupla slabs and he'll do us up a feed. Reckons him and Flash, and Fleabag if he wants, will drive out ta Moonkoo Station the next day and git a fresh sheep. We know Flea's up for it. He gits on well with Unc and Flash cos they let him sit up front in the car with em and when they get to wherever it is they're going he gits to run round and chase rabbits, swim in dams, roll in dead stuff and act like a proper dog. Trouble is, that night it rains and rains. Just pisses down, turnin the red dust into red clay and cos all the roads leadin in and out of our town are dirt, no cars are goin anywhere.

Uncle Ronnie comes round in the mornin to bring us the bad news. Reckons it'll be a few days before he can git out to Moonkoo, but says he'll bite the bullet and go and buy a sheep off that robbin bastard of a butcher, Old Billy Sullivan, on account me, Ant and Fleabag have gotta leave on Monday to git back to the city for work and shit.

So we all pile into his ute, Flash and Flea sittin on our laps, and head down to the butcher shop.

Me and Ant and the dogs wait on the nature strip on the other side of the road while Unc goes in to buy the meat.

Next thing we hear Unc yellin. 'Listen you robbin mongrel. If I'm payin that much for a sheep, the fuckin thing better have golden fleece and platinum balls.'

He comes stormin outta the shop. 'Stick ya fuckin sheep up ya arse. You're nothin but a legalised bandit.'

'C'mon you fullas,' Unc reckons. 'Git in the car.'

We see Billy Sullivan standin in the doorway of the shop with his legs crossed at the ankles and suckin on a long neck a beer.

'Well Ronnie Harris,' he yells out ta Unc. 'If you don't like the prices, you can always go to the other butcher shop.' He waves his free hand down the empty street with a big, smart-arse grin on his face.

Unc turns round. 'You better git your fat arse back inside before I come over and knock your fuckin head clean off ya fuckin shoulders.'

Before you can say 'tucker's on', Flash and Flea are at Unc's side, ready to back im up if a blue happens. But Billy Sullivan's back inside his filthy old shop before ya know it. Everyone round these parts knows ya don't pick on Ronnie Harris. He's a wiry old tent boxer, tough as nails and he's flogged heaps a young blokes twice his size and half his age. Besides, ya not just fightin Unc, ya gotta take on Flash as well. And he don't take too kindly to fullas pickin on his mate.

Anyway, next thing we hear this voice yellin, 'Hey, Ronnie Harris. Whatcha bungin on with Billy Sullivan for? Come over and have a drink with me.'

We look over. It's Old Mother Howard. She's sittin

on her verandah drinkin port out of a flagon and smokin rollies. She's as ugly as sin, is Old Mother Howard. Skinniest woman ya ever saw. She's got hair that's flat and greasy and the same colour as that grey shit ya git outta blocked up drains. She's got beady, little blue eyes that are always waterin up, teeth all crooked and stained from tobacco and port wine, and flaky, grey skin she's always pickin at.

She's married to Old Mick Howard. He's big and fat, with red hair, red face, piggy blue eyes and an extra finger and toe on each hand and foot. They got six bony, ugly kids, all with red hair, and all of em have got the extra fingers and toes. The fullas down at the Rotary Club wanted to raise money to git the extra toes and fingers taken off, but Old Mick reckons it's what God give him and his kids and they aint got no problem with it.

Dad reckons if Old Mick had half a brain it'd be lonely. He also reckons God gives ya boils on ya arse, but ya do ya best ta git rid of em.

But Ma reckons ya gotta hand it to Old Mick, cos he loves and looks after those kids. If they didn't have their father, Ma reckons the welfare would've taken those poor kids away years ago on account of their drunken, useless mother.

The Howards are whitefullas and not related to our mob, but all the blackfullas look out for the kids cos they feel sorry for the little buggers. Ma and Dad give em biscuits and cordial to take with em to play and Aunty Pearlie's always givin Old Mick big jars of vitamin E cream to rub on their scaly skin. She says it might stop em from itching so much. Uncle Ronnie gives em meat too. Reckon it'd only go ta waste otherwise.

Anyway me, Antman, Unc and the dogs walk over the road to talk to Mother Howard. She's been pickin at her skin and the flakes are layin all around her. It looks just like ashes after a bush fire. Me and Ant look at one another and back down the stairs but Unc walks right up to her.

She looks up at im from her old couch and passes im the flagon. 'Have a little drink, Ronnie. It'll calm ya down. Seems like you got your black balls in a knot over somethin.'

'No thanks, Jeannie,' reckons Uncle Ronnie. 'I'm drivin and I got me niece and her fulla with me. Maybe next time.'

'Ya weak as piss, Ronnie Harris. Anyway, what's goin on?'

'I wanted to git a sheep from out Moonkoo and put on a camp oven do but the roads are too muddy. Won't git a motor car through for a coupla days. So I tried to buy a sheep at the butcher's but that robbin bastard saw me comin. He wants a fortune for his ratty old meat so I told im to stick it up his arse. Dunno what I'm gunna do now.'

'Well,' says Mother Howard. 'I gotta sheep out the back ya can have. I'll let it go for two flagons and packet a tobacca.'

'I'll wanna have a look at it first,' reckons Unc.

'Help yaself,' she says, draggin on her rollie and peelin off another piece of dead skin.

Me and Antman shiver.

So Unc and Flash go and check out the sheep. Unc reckons it'll have to do and gits Antman to go and buy the grog and smoko.

Unc reckons he'll put the sheep in the ute and take it home, but Old Mother Howard reckons she'll send the kids round with it later, on account of she don't know where the rope is. Unc reckons okay. But he says, 'Don't fuck me up, Jeannie. I want that sheep today and there'll be no grog and tobacco till I git it.'

Old Mother Howard promises she won't fuck with im and says he'll have it in half an hour.

So we git back to Unc's camp and he sends me over to git Dad and tell him to fetch his meat bag and hooks and bring back his sharp killin knife.

So I go back over with Dad, and then him, Antman and Unc start gittin things ready to kill the sheep.

Next thing, two of the Howard kids turn up with the sheep on a rope. It's one of the little girls, about eight and a boy around ten. Cos they all look alike, no one knows who's who so they just git called the Howard Kids.

Unc gives em the tobacco and grog and tells em thanks. But the little girl's cryin. 'Ya better give us back the rope, Mr Harris. Mum's gunna kill us if we don't bring back the rope.'

Unc takes the rope off and hands it to the little girl. She and her brother go over and throw their arms around the sheep and then they both start cryin. The little girl's goin, 'Bye, bye Myrtle. We'll see ya in heaven one day.'

Dad and Unc look at one other. 'Whut are you little fullas cryin for?' Dad asks. 'It's only a sheep.'

The little boy looks at em. 'She aint just a sheep, Mr Harris. She's Myrtle and she's our pet sheep. Dad give her to us a coupla years ago.'

The little girl chips in. 'We love her, Mr Harris. Dad's gunna git real cranky with Ma when he finds out she got Myrtle kilt.'

And they both start wailin again.

Dad and Unc look at one other. 'Poor little buggers,' Dad says.

Unc gits down on his knees and tells them two Howard kids to stop cryin cos he's gotta plan.

Dad gives em his clean hanky to wipe their eyes. When they try to give it back to im he reckons no, they can keep it. Anyway, when they stop cryin they look at Unc and ask im about his plan.

'Well, I'll tell youse what. Myrtle can live here with me and Flash. And all you kids can come by everyday or whenever you want to visit her. I'll build her a little place to keep the rain off and she can keep the lawn nice and tidy. What do youse reckon about that, aye?'

Their little, beady, watery eyes light up and they reckon it's great. The little fulla reckons his Ma would only sell Myrtle to someone else anyway. So Unc gives em the rope, the flagons and the tobacco and they skip home happy as can be.

Unc pulls outta big heap a money and gives it to me and Ant and sends us down to the butcher's ta git a sheep.

Next day we have the big camp oven do. All us blackfullas sittin round chewin on good tucker, havin a beer, listenin to Slim Dusty and tellin lies.

Flash, Flea and Dad's dog, Humbug, are havin a big gorge on sheep bones and Myrtle's wanderin around with a big ribbon in the Koori colours round her neck, eatin the lawn like there's no tomorrer.

Unc's whingin ta Dad about the chemical taste in the meat.

'Don't go complainin ta me, brother,' Dad says. 'It's ya own fault. Ya always was weak as piss, Ronnie Harris.'

The Grub

One time, when me, Antman and Fleabag got sick of livin and workin in the city, we went out home to do some work in the shearin sheds. I do some rouseaboutin, Ant does some cookin and Flea does whatever he wants.

Me sister Lulla's married to a shearin contractor called Rick and he always puts together a team of all blackfullas. We're usually related and we have the best time. We work hard durin the day, then after we have a shower we sit round and have a coupla beers, then a feed and another coupla beers and then bed. It's a good life out in the back country, nice and quiet.

Anyway, last time we went out, there was this fulla. Me and Ant aint never seen im before. He sat on his own, away from everyone else. He'd git his own tucker and go and eat it outside, he'd drink his beer on his own too.

I asked Lulla how come he did that. I thought he was one of them stuck up blackfullas, she reckoned no, he just liked bein on his own. She also told me he wasn't a blackfulla. I was a bit surprised cos he sure looked like one from a distance.

Then Cousin Yogi puts his two bob's worth in. 'He's that colour cos he don't wash. He aint had a tub in years. Just as well he sits on his own. Ya wouldn't wanna git too close too im. One time he was asleep out over near the paddock and I swear to gawd the dogs was rollin in im. The crows and eagles were circlin round im too.'

Lulla reckons Yogi was right about the washin bit, but he was goin too far with the bit about the dogs and the birds.

Rick reckoned Yogi was speakin the truth cos he seen it himself. He said he was a really good presser though, and as long as he did his job, he could always git work with his team.

All that week we never saw that fulla go near a tap. He slept in a hut on his own and at night he would walk out to the long drop toilet and sit there for hours playin Bob Dylan on the mouth organ. He wasn't bad either and cos it was so quiet in the wide open saltbush country, the music would float over to where the rest of us fullas were and sometimes we'd sing along.

His name's Trevor Mitchell, but we call him 'the Grub'. No one knows where he came from, if he has a wife, family or anything. He just drifted into town one day in his beat up old Torana lookin for work pressin.

Rick was desperate and give him a start. Some of the fullas used to complain bout the smell, but funny thing is, after a while ya git used to it. Besides, most of the time he don't come close enough to a body for ya to notice. And like Rick says, he's real good at his job. A coupla other contractors have tried to pinch him, but he's loyal to Rick. Been with him for ages.

So we did the week and cut out from the shed on the Friday and was headin into town to cash our cheques and git pissed. Yogi was travellin with us and cos he lost a fight with Fleabag for the front seat, was sittin in the back suckin on a long neck, sulkin and carryin on about spoilt, fuckin city dogs and not letting up bout how me and Antman encourage Flea to be an arsehole. Ant give Flea a biscuit and a pat and said he don't need no encouraging; he can be an arsehole all on his own. That really give Yogi the shits.

Anyway, me and Ant starts talkin bout how dirty the Grub is.

I said I couldn't believe anyone could live their life without havin a wash. I mean there aint nothin better after a hard day's workin, than standin under a shower and lettin it wash all the sweat and grime away.

Then Antman reckons he'd have to be lousy. Reckons he'd be crawlin with lice.

Yogi pipes up from the back. 'No way, Ant. Those lice would perish for sure.'

'Whadda ya mean they'd perish?'

'No fuckin water.'

Me and Ant looked at another and reckoned, 'Yeh, aye!'

The counter lunch

One time me, Antman and Fleabag was travellin out to do some work in the shearin sheds.

Anyway, we come to this little back country town and see this little pub (the only pub) with a big old sign out the front sayin 'COUNTER LUNCH SERVED INSIDE'. There's a coupla utes parked out the front under the trees with dogs sittin alongside em, patiently waitin for their mates inside.

Ant parks the car cos it was just what we was lookin for. We was hangin for one of them old-style counter lunches. Big steaks or cutlets, served with proper old-fashioned lettuce, beetroot, orange slice, onions, and that cheese ya can roll up, and all drownin in vinegar.

So we gits out and Ant pours some water for Flea and gives him a bone. The heat's got to the dogs beside the utes and they can't even be arsed barkin at Flea, let alone pickin a blue, so we leave him to it and go inside.

There's cracked lino on the floors, pictures of the big flood over the bar and a few outback paintins done on plywood shaped into the map of Australia. It's air-conditioned too, nice and cool. There's a coupla fullas in the bar, just drinkin and starin into space. They look at us and go back to wherever they was before we got there. The barmaid's a tiny old woman wearin a black skirt, black shoes, stockins and white shirt. She only looks up from the magazine she's readin when Ant orders a coupla coldies and asks her what she thinks bout the heat. She reckons it was hot enough ta scorch the feathers off a duck's arse. We agree and cruise over to check out the jukebox. There's country music and more country music, which suits me and Ant just fine, so we put a coupla Charlie Pride, Slim and Merle Haggard songs on.

We sit down and are lookin for a menu, but we can't see one. Ant reckons they probably only serve a coupla things, but says they're sure to have steak and salad.

Anyway, we finish our beers and decide to order. So we walk back over to the bar to tell the barmaid what we want.

'We'd like to order a couple of steaks and salad,' Ant says. 'And we'll have a coupla more beers while we wait.'

She looks at us like we was from the moon. 'What steaks and salads?'

Ant tells her bout the sign out front advertisin counter lunches and says again that we'd like to order a couple. He reckons it was okay if they had no steak, we'd just have whatever was on the menu.

She give us that same blank look again. 'We don't have counter lunches in here, luv.'

'What do ya mean? You fullas have got a big sign out the front sayin counter lunch served here.'

'Oh that,' she says, flickin over a page of the magazine. 'That sign's been out there for years. We aint had counter lunches in here since Noah was a baby. Aint that right, boys?'

The two fullas agree with her and go back to their beers.

Ant asks if they serve any tucker in the pub at all.

She reckons they got chips. Plain, chicken or salt and vinegar.

We git a packet of each. Least we can say we had spuds with chicken and vinegar for lunch. They tasted all right too, washed down with a few beers and some good country on the jukebox.

The funeral goer

Cousin Moodle loves funerals. She don't care whose funeral it is, she goes anyway. She's always ridin on the funeral bus to some place or another. Funeral buses are usually hired. Or if the Land Council's gotta bus, they use them to take people to towns to pay their respects.

Sometimes when a funeral bus is passin through town, Moodle packs a bag and goes along with em if they got the room. They can usually squeeze someone else on.

Moodle loves makin a big fuss and bein the centre of attention at funerals. She gits dressed up to the nines in her fancy, black funeral rig-out and hat. She wails and weeps and likes to be helped in and out of the church by at least two people. She likes to stumble and sometimes she faints. The way she carries on really gives Dad the shits and sometimes he tells her to wake up to herself and stop carryin on like some fuckin demented idiot.

Ma reckons Dad should have a bit of patience with Moodle. She reckons Moodle aint hurtin no one. Besides, Ma reckons blackfullas like a bit of a show at these things cos they like talkin bout how old so-and-so carried on afterwards. Especially when they're sittin round havin their tea and cakes and sandwiches.

One of the things Moodle likes to do is run towards the coffin as it's bein lowered into the ground, yellin stuff like, 'Please Lord, take me with her'. People grab her just before she jumps. Dad reckons she relies on them to grab her in time.

Anyway, one time Moodle goes to this funeral. It'd been rainin for days and the red clay was slippery and ya had ta watch what you was doin so ya didn't slip or nothin. Moodle gits carried away as usual as they start lowerin the coffin and starts runnin towards it screamin, 'Lord, Gawd Almighty, please take me with him.'

Only one of the fullas slips and doesn't catch her in time. Then Moodle slips herself and goes slidin into the grave, landing right on top of the coffin that's been lowered halfway down.

So Moodle's sittin on the coffin wailin. 'But please Lord, Gawd Almighty, not now, not now. I aint ready to go just yet.'

Suddenly everyone's rushin over there helpin Moodle outta the grave.

Ma whispers to Dad that he should go over and help too but he reckons may as well leave her there cos it might teach her a lesson.

It didn't though. She still gets dressed to the nines and goes to every funeral she can. And she still wails and runs at the coffin. Only difference is now she always makes sure someone's there and all ready to catch her in time.

The golden wedding anniversary

Me, Antman and Fleabag went to Uncle Vic and Aunty Bess's fiftieth wedding anniversary. They're Ant's relations. It was a great party. All Aunty Bess's mob came. Uncle Vic's brother, his wife, kids, their kids and hundreds of their friends. Their only child Della came from Brisbane with husband Chris and two children, thirteen-year-old Buddy and ten-year-old Lulu.

They had Old Merv Hanrahan as master of ceremonies. Ant reckons he emcees every local event, from christenings, to funerals, engagements to weddings, presentations, sporting or otherwise. He got the job years ago cos he owned a suit and was never lost for words. Uncle Vic reckoned Merv had an opinion on everything and everyone, whether you wanted it or not. Also, his wife Dulcie made the best wine trifle in the district and always brought one along, so that didn't hurt either.

The Dandenong Country Drifters were the band for the night. They played country, rock-and-roll and some waltzes for the older folk, and pretty soon had everyone up dancing. The first one up was Luvvo. Coal black skin, a shock of white hair and the figure of someone twenty years younger, Luvvo could shake it with the best of them. And when she'd throw back her head and yell in her port wine and cigarette growl, 'I still got it', no one doubted her, least of all the women, young or old. They kept their men folk real close when Luvvo was around.

Later in the evening Bess and Vic danced the Anniversary Waltz. Vic, tall, fair, blue-eyed and sandy-haired. Bess, tiny and dark, with long, thick hair, black but for a few streaks of silver that gave off a sparkle as she danced lightly in his arms. They looked as in love today as they were fifty years ago when they married in the old registry with her mum and dad and his granny looking on.

Then came the speeches. Different ones got up and talked about what a great couple they were. They talked about how they'd turned their property into the best in the district. About their generosity, their terrific family. Della spoke about what fantastic parents they were, how much she and her husband and kids loved and were so proud of them. Vic and Bess was fairly lit up with pride.

Finally Vic got up. He thanked everyone – from his friends, family and the Lord for his wonderful life and the gift of Bess, Della and her family. He and everyone else spoke about everything. Everything but what Della really wanted to hear.

Antman reckoned she'd pestered em for years.

'Please,' she'd beg. 'Tell me how you met. I tell everyone how I met Chris at uni. How we fell in love. How he proposed.'

But they'd just say, 'It doesn't matter.' Or tell her, 'It's in the past. We're together now. That's all that matters.'

She'd ask their friends or relatives but they'd go quiet. Tell her it wasn't up to them to say. Reckoned Vic and Bess would tell her when they were ready. It drove her mad. She'd moan about it to Chris, or me and Ant, and we'd say they probably had their reasons. That just give her the shits.

After the party, Big Jim West (five foot four in his socks) drove us all home. He'd been the town drunk, proppin up the bar of the Royal Mail from openin to half past drunk for many years. Then he met Ollie who fell in love with the man, not the drunk. Reckoned he was a good sort, just needed sprucin up. She got him sober and he hasn't touched a drop in twenty years. Non-drinkers were a rarity in these parts, and it wasn't long before he became 'designated driver', the town eventually purchasing a community bus of which Big Jim was supreme overlord.

The bus belted along the dirt and gravel moonlit roads. People, full of grog and good cheer, sang out of tune as each family was dropped off in turn, until finally all us mob. We was stayin with Unc and Aunt. Uncle Vic, Chris and Ant went ta bed, they was pretty pissed, so me, Aunty Bess and Della sat out on the wide, screened verandah and sipped cold beer.

'Jeez, Ma, it was a beaut party,' reckoned Della.

'The best thing was you, Chris and the kids comin home,' replied Bess.

'Wouldn't have missed it. Luvvo can still shake it, aye?' said Della, sipping her beer.

'You're not wrong, daught. I told her she better keep her paws off your father, or me and her will be knucklin up.'

'Oh, Ma! Luvvo'd make mincemeat of you,' laughed Della.

Bess chuckled. 'Don't bet on it, bubby. Ya father's worth fightin for.'

We just sat there all quiet, just listenin to the sound of crickets.

Finally Della spoke. 'Ma, please tell me how you met. It can't be that bad.'

'Leave it alone, daught.'

Then the low rumble of Vic's voice disturbed us. We hadn't heard him come out.

'Tell her, Bess. It's about time.'

'Gawd, Vic! Sneakin up like that. You sure?'

'I'm sure. We'll both tell her.'

I said maybe I should go inside and leave em in peace but they reckoned no, I could stay if I wanted.

Vic sat beside Bess and took her tiny, dark hand in his, and after a deep breath, Bess started speaking.

'In those days, men had no respect for us Koori girls. They'd come sneakin round camps at night, bringin grog. Stirrin up trouble. Sometimes they'd chase us home from town. They got one of me cousins. She killed herself not long after. Funny thing though, the day after they did it, they was all down town with their women folk, helpin em with their shoppin, actin right and proper, tippin their hats to all the white ladies. Meanwhile Ruthie's lying bleedin in a hospital bed and no copper would believe her story. Even if they did, they wouldn't have charged em. They were white, we was black, end of story. Who do you reckon the cops believed? After that, men from the camp would go everywhere with us.'

Bess sipped her beer and looked at Vic who squeezed her hand. She took a deep breath and continued.

'Anyway, I had a job in town, cleanin the café. One day me brother was late pickin me up. I got impatient, started walkin home by meself. I was halfway there when I heard the truck. It was drivin slow and I turned around and saw it comin across the paddock. I heard the boys yahooin and laughin. I knew I was in trouble.

'I started runnin so fast I thought me heart was gunna burst. I zigzagged across the paddock, like Ma told me. She reckoned it slowed em down long enough to get away. But it wasn't workin and I tripped over a log and fell down. I thought, I'm gone, they're gunna kill me.

'I heard the truck stop. I heard em yahooin. Then I heard the doors slam. I was prayin to the Lord to get me outta this mess. Promised I would always wait for my brother. Would always do the right thing if he'd save me.

'Then I heard an almighty bang. It was a rifle. I thought they'd kill me right there. They wouldn't just rape me; they'd kill me. Then I thought bugger it, I'm not gunna lay here with me face in the dirt and let em shoot me in the back like a mongrel dog. They was gunna have to look me in the face before they done it. I turned over, and I saw Merv and Big Jim and a couple of other blokes from town. Ya father was standin there with the rifle pointed at em. They was tellin him to calm down. Big Jim was sayin, "She's only a gin. They love it, mate."

'I sat up and looked at em. Then I heard ya father say, "Look at her. She's just a kid. You mob of animals git back in the truck and piss off before I blow ya heads clean off."

'Merv, Jim and the others got back in the truck. Merv was givin ya father cheek. He was sayin he was weak as piss. Accused him of goin soft, of turnin on his mates for an Abo. Ya father told em to piss off. He wasn't muckin round anymore and fired another shot in the air. They got into the truck and took off, still yellin cheek at ya father.

'He walked over to me and, somehow, I just knew it was gunna be okay.'

Della's face was white. Tears were streaming down her face. Even if she had wanted to speak, she wouldn't have been able too. She was struck dumb by what she was hearing. Vic continued the story.

'Gawd I felt like a bastard. Stupid too. The lads asked me to go huntin. I thought they meant for wild pigs or roos. When they saw Bess walkin and started yellin "there's one, let's git her." I couldn't believe it. I was tellin em to wake up to their selves. But they wouldn't take any notice.

'Big Jim kept drivin like a maniac. Then Bessie fell

and Jim stopped the truck. They jumped out and I knew what they were gunna do. I couldn't let it happen so I grabbed me rifle and fired it into the air. They were full of cheek, but like the cowards they were, they weren't gunna take the chance so they left. I walked over to ya mother. She looked so little and helpless, but she seemed to trust me so that when I put the gun down and offered her me hand, she took it and I helped her stand up. She was shakin and terrified. Then I looked into the brownest eyes I've ever seen. I knew there and then I'd marry her. No matter what, Bess was gunna be my wife.

'While we were standin there a mob arrived from her camp. They were in a panic. They thought someone had been shot. They saw me and ya mother. Saw the shotgun on the ground. I explained what had happened. Told how em how sorry I was. How ashamed I was. Bess's dad asked me back to the camp for a cuppa. Told me I was a bigger man than those mongrels would ever be.

'Then I started goin back all the time. Just to visit Bess. I remember the first day I drove her and me to the pictures. Everyone was lookin at us. In those days they made Aboriginal people sit in a roped-off section of the theatre. So I sat with her there.'

Bessie squeezed his hand and continued on with the story.

'The manager came up and told him that he shouldn't sit there. It was for the Abos. He said he was with me and if I couldn't sit in the other section then he wasn't gunna either. Gawd we copped some shit. We'd walk up the street and blokes would call him a gin jockey. He wanted to belt em, but I wouldn't let him. He'd just wind up in gaol. They weren't worth it.

'Then he asked me to marry him. I told him he was off his rocker. I didn't mind if he just came and visited me, took me out. But I told him he'd be better off marrying a white girl. I told him his family would hit the roof. He said he didn't care.

'And she was right, baby girl,' said Vic. 'I didn't care. She was then, and she still is, the only girl for me.

'I asked her father for her hand, he said yes, but he warned us of the hard road ahead. I took her home and me folks hit the roof. Said they'd cut me outta the will. I'd git nothin. But me old grandma said me and Bess could have her old property. She reckoned we could make a go of it. She loved Bess from the day she met her. And we did make a go of it. Together we made it the best sheep station around. Then you come along and well, everything's been great.'

Della looked at them.

'How could you forgive Old Merv and Big Jim? How could you speak to those animals let alone be their friends? There was Merv talking at the party about what a wonderful couple you are. How great Mum is. He's nothing but a fucking hypocrite.'

Bess took Della's hand and quietly said, 'Darlin, I didn' bring you up to use language like that.'

'What do you mean language like that?' screamed Della. 'Those men are pigs!'

Vic stood up and walked over to the edge of the verandah and after what seemed an eternity said, 'I don't expect you to understand, but when we got married something came over Merv. He came over one day with Dulcie. She had a trifle with her. Ya ma asked em in and Merv stood there with his hat in his hand and he asked for our forgiveness. Said it had been preyin on his mind. Dulcie reckoned he'd been evil, but he should say sorry and ask for forgiveness and even if we refused, at least he'd tried to be a decent man and make up for what he done.

'I said it was up to ya ma. She was cryin and said of course she'd forgive him. We cracked a couple of bottles of beer and we've been friends ever since. Through thick and thin. Hatred gets ya nowhere, bubby. I thought we'd taught you that.

'Big Jim felt bad too. But he took to the drink until he got married. Even then it took a few years for him to say he was sorry. They were the only two that did. None of the other boys did. But we didn't and we still don't need em in our lives, bubby.'

Bess stood up and taking Vic's hand said, 'It's time we was goin to bed. You need time to think things through, bub. Just remember, me and ya father had the best marriage. We wouldn't change a thing. A lot of women never find the measure of their men. I saw his the minute I met him. It doesn't matter how we met. What matters is that we met.'

Della sat in the dark for a long time after. I sat there

with her, just holdin her hand. Hot, salty tears were soaking her face and dampening the crisp, white cotton of her party dress. She couldn't get over what had happened and kept askin why.

She felt angry that her beautiful mother had gone through such brutality. And worse, it had been at the hands of men she had known and trusted all her life. She asked me how she could look at them in the same way anymore. I reckoned I didn't know.

Then she felt a strong hand on her shoulder and looked up at the sad face of her husband.

'You heard?' she asked.

'Yeh. Let it go, Dell. It was their decision to forgive. It's nothing to do with you.'

Della told me the next day that she wanted to scream at him. Ask him if he could understand how she felt. But in her heart she knew that he was right. Anger was their prerogative, not hers. She wiped the tears from her eyes with the hem of her dress, took his hand and said, 'Let's go to bed. It's been a long night.'

I reckoned it had.

Ma and Dad's big trip

Me Ma and Dad went on the Indian Pacific and the Ghan up to Alice Springs. It was first class all the way.

They had a fancy cabin and they ate all their meals in the flash dinin room. All the way from home to Alice and back again they was drinkin top shelf grog and there was a chef preparin four-star tucker. Most of it looked just like that food ya see in them flash magazines or on them cookin shows on the telly.

Anyway, after a coupla days, Ma got sick of eatin all that fine food. Hated all the sauces and the way they stacked everything up. She used to git wild when they put her meat on top of the chips. 'What stupid bastard come up with that idea? Don't they know it makes the chips soggy?' She reckoned the tucker was so fancy ya couldn't tell what the fuck you was eatin half the time.

Anyway, this day she's had a gutful so when the waiter comes up and asks em what they was havin for lunch, Dad orders up fancy like a big man. Then the waiter turns to Ma and says, 'And what would madam like to eat today?'

Ma looks up at him and says in her sweetest voice, 'Well, ya know, I wouldn' mind havin somethin nice and simple. You know, like chops, tomato and some lettuce.'

The waiter looks at Ma. 'I'll see what I can do, Mrs Harris. I can't promise anything, but I'm sure our chef would only be too happy to accommodate you.'

'I'm sorry to be a nuisance,' Ma replies, 'but I would appreciate it, luv.'

So the waiter comes back with the tucker. He's got Dad's fancy feed of Veal Provencale with herb and cream noodles and a warm side salad. And for Ma he's got a rack of lamb, some cherry tomatoes and a handful of rocket. He bungs it down in front of her with a flourish.

'There you go, Mrs Harris. I think you'll enjoy that.'

After the waiter leaves, Ma looks down at the tucker in disgust and starts pokin at it and movin it round on her plate.

'Look at the size of these fuckin tomatoes, will ya?' she says to Dad. 'And what kinda lettuce is this supposed ta be?'

'I dunno, Beryl. Anyway, stop makin a fuss and eat the fuckin thing.'

'I don't think I will,' Ma reckons. 'I mean, Roy, we paid a lotta money to come on this trip. Ya think they could serve up some decent size tomatoes. And another thing,' she says, turnin the racks of lamb this way and that, 'would it have killed em to cut up the chops?'

★

One time, on the trip they took to Alice, Ma and Dad decide to go and visit Coober Pedy. They visit all the underground museums and shops. They fossick for opals and drink beer in the pub and mingle with the locals.

One fulla asks Ma if she and Dad was gunna stay in the underground hotel for the night.

No way, Ma reckons. She's gunna have to spend the rest of her life underground when she's dead.

Shoppin with Aunty Pearlie

Aunty Pearlie, Dad's sister, is one of those flash blackfullas. Always goin on bout what a good name she has. Always sayin stuff like, 'Everyone respects me in this town. When I walk up the street they say, "Hello, Mrs Johnson. How are you today?" I always say, "Good thanks, love. Thanks for asking." It doesn't cost anything to be polite.'

Aunty Pearlie always gits dressed up to the nines in flowery dresses, stockins and shoes. Even if she's just goin down the street for a pint of milk. She's a big woman with long grey hair she wears in a plait. She's as black as can be, but she always wears a hat when she goes out. If it's the middle of summer, she takes an umbrella to keep the sun off her. She loves a yarn too, does Aunty. Dad reckons she's the greatest lug basher around. Reckons she could talk a dog off a meat wagon.

Aunty Pearlie's always goin on about doin things proper, includin speakin. Trouble is, she gits fucked up all the time. One time she was whingin to Dad about how expensive Old Billy Sullivan the butcher was. She was goin on about the price of this and the price of that. Then she says, 'You know what, brother?'

'What, Sister Pearl?' says Dad, rollin his eyes.

'That bandit had the cheek to charge me ten dollars for a kilometre's worth of sausages!'

We still laugh over that one.

She's always goin on at us bout the way we talk. She hates us sayin 'blackfullas'. Reckons it's 'blackfellows'. And anyway, she reckons we shouldn't call ourselves that. 'We're Aborigines', she says. She's always correctin us for sayin 'nothin' and 'somethin' and 'goin'. She says, 'It's "nothing", "something", "going".'

She tries to get us to repeat those words with her. We do cos it makes her happy and it makes Dad laugh. He reckons he don't know how she got to be so flash. Reckons she watched too many Greer Garson and Katharine Hepburn movies when she was a kid.

Even her dog, Missy, is flash. She's white and fluffy as can be. All the other dogs round the place are covered in red dust, but you don't see a speck on Missy. She's mean though. Our mutt Fleabag don't like her. She towelled him up proper when we was visitin a couple of years ago. Now, he crosses the road whenever he sees her comin, and when we visit Aunty Pearlie he stays outside, under a tree if it's hot, or in the car if it's cold. Dad used ta reckon Flea was weak as piss for lettin Missy stand over him. Then she gives his dog Humbug a tune-up. Now Humbug sits outside with Flea and Dad don't say nothin.

One thing Aunty Pearlie loves to do is go down to old Clarrie Barraclough's store every pension day to do her shoppin. It's the only store in town. One side is the grocery and hardware part. Old Clarrie runs that. The other side is where you buy clothes, presents, material and stuff and old Mrs Garraway, or Mrs G as everyone calls her, runs that. After Aunty's bought groceries out the front, she goes out the back for a yarn with old Mrs G and to buy stuff like new hankies, or tea towels or presents for someone or other.

Aunty Pearlie reckons Mrs Garraway is a real lady and even though they've only ever spoken in the store, Aunty likes to think of her as a friend. Always goin on about them havin so much in common, both of em bein widows and all.

Aunty's been a widow for a few years now. Uncle Dave just up and died one day. He was watchin a video of *Bonanza* on the telly and pretendin to listen to Aunty. She reckons she asked im if he was ready for his supper and he didn't answer. She reckon she got wild with him for not listenin to her when she was speaking and when she leant over to yell at im, she realised he was dead. Dad reckons Aunty talked the poor old fulla to death.

Ma says she's got her doubts about old Mrs G bein a widow though. Reckons she just turned up one day with a little baby on the mail truck. They was on their way to Cobar. She was waitin outside the store while the truck refuelled and she saw a sign lookin for help in the store and she went in and next thing ya know she's workin in there and livin in the old flat out the back with her baby girl.

One day, about five years later, a big, flash car turns up and a couple of old whitefullas in fancy clothes gits out and goes and talks to Mrs G. Next thing ya know she's buyin her own house and sendin her little girl off to some fancy school in the city. Ma reckons they come and bought her off.

Aunty gits her bloomers in a right twist over that. Reckons it's no one's business and when Ma says, 'if she's a widow then my arse is white,' Aunty's eyeballs pop out and the veins in her neck near burst.

Anyway, Aunty likes to say real loud in the grocery section that she's just 'ducking' round the back to visit 'her friend' Mrs Garraway.

Old Mrs G's real skinny, with stiff purple hair that don't move. Not even when she's walkin in a willy-willy. Dad reckons even a cyclone couldn't move that hair. She's got a long, thin face and a nose to match. Her skin's kinda grey-coloured, and she wears black skirts and twin sets in winter and brown skirts and white cotton shirts done up at the collar in summer. It don't matter how hot it is, she always wears stockins and lace-up shoes.

No one's ever seen Mrs G laugh, smile or cry. Only thing she does is raise her left eyebrow sometimes. And Aunty Pearlie gits that eyebrow workin all the time.

When me and Antman visit, we like to go down to the store with Aunty Pearlie. We specially like bein with her when she goes to see old Mrs G. She always snaps at us to behave ourselves and not 'touch anything' or interrupt her when she's 'talking'.

Anyway, last time we was home we went with her. We helped her with the groceries, then we went out the back so she could visit Mrs G. Aunty Pearlie sweeps into the store like a big old black queen and says in her most hoity-toity voice, 'Good morning, Mrs Garraway. How are you today?'

'Very well, Mrs Johnson. And your good lady self?' says Mrs G.

Aunty Pearlie grows a coupla feet on account of Mrs G calling her a lady and says, 'I'm doing as well as can be expected in this hot heat. It must be around 40 centimetres in the shade. But thanks for asking.'

Mrs G's eyebrow shoots up. 'You're very welcome, I'm sure. And I have to agree, the heat is rather enervating.'

'You must be more used to it than me, Mrs Garraway, I just find it drains the life clean out of me. Anyway, did you hear the Flying Doctor come in this morning?'

'Yes I did. I believe ...' Mrs G starts.

But Aunty cuts her off. She likes to be the one tellin the story.

'Well,' says Aunty, 'they came for Old Norm Hunt. He went to the clinic the other day and they sent him home with some aspirin. Said he had the flu. Anyway, his wife took him up to the hospital at two o'clock this morning and Sister Chapman radioed the Flying Doctors and they reckon he had all the simpsoms of remonia and sent a plane to fetch him straightaway.'

Mrs G's left eyebrow shoots up again and she says, 'Yes I heard he had pneumonia. Very dangerous thing to have is pneumonia.'

'Yes. Old Mrs Mac died from remonia last year,' reckons Aunty.

Me and Antman were about ready to bust out laughin but we held it in. We knew the show wasn't over.

'So, Mrs Johnson. What can I get for you today?' says Mrs G.

'Well,' says Aunt, 'I've been thinking about making myself some new frocks for summer, so I'll need to look at material. It's so expensive to buy clothes and I used to be able to sew quite well in my younger years.'

So Mrs G gets down some material and Aunty makes a big show of lookin it over. Then she tells Mrs G how much she wants.

'And while I'm here I'd better get a couple of reels of white cotting.'

'I beg your pardon, Mrs Johnson?'

'Sorry, Mrs G. I'll have a couple of reels of white cotting, please,' replies Aunty.

Old Mrs G's eyebrow shoots up so far it nearly flies fair off her face, but she gets the white cotton reels and places them in front of Aunt.

It was too much for me and Ant. We run outside and fell down on the nature strip and just busted our guts laughin. Fleabag was jumpin all over us, joinin in the fun, when Aunt walked out with her packages. She stopped dead in her tracks and looked at us lyin on the grass.

'Hmmppph,' she snapped at us. 'Just look at you lot. Lying around on the ground like a pack of mongrel dogs. It's behaviour like that gives the rest of us Aboriginal people a bad name. Are you coming with me?'

We reckoned no. Said we'd walk home. She told us to suit ourselves and got in her car and drove off.

We got up and tried to catch our breath and was lookin in through the big old glass windows at Mrs G's counter. She was shakin and wipin her eyes. Antman reckoned she must have had some bad news just after servin us and we opened the door to see if she needed help. When we got in we realised she wasn't cryin. She was laughin so hard it was like she was gunna piss herself. We just turned round and left her to it. We run all the way home to tell Dad.

The water skiers

Me, Antman and Fleabag was in the river country visitin Antman's mob.

We was stayin with Antman's uncle, Old Billy Swindle. He lives on the riverbank with his dog, Kooru, and his goat, Mona Lisa. He was born there, under a tree. He aint never left. He's got a little caravan to sleep in and a tin shelter that's got a table, chairs, a kerosene fridge and a portable gas stove. He's got a battery radio, a guitar and a dartboard.

Old Billy aint never had a job cos he don't pay rent. He grows his own veggies, catches his own meat and fish and Mona Lisa gives him plenty of milk. If he needs cash he traps some foxes and sells the pelts. Everyone's been tryin for years to git im ta go and live in town.

'C'mon, Unc,' all his mob says to him. 'We'll git you a nice little flat. Everything's inside. Ya can have a little garden if ya want.'

He's even run a coupla social workers off his camp with a shotgun in the past when they was tryin to tell him it would be best if he lived in town. He reckoned he'd be the fuckin judge of what was best for him. Those fullas got a bit windy of him after that and pretty well left him alone. Suited Unc just fine.

Seems Uncle Billy told em ta stick their flats up their arses. He reckons it's livin in little boxes where ya shit and piss inside where ya supposed to be eatin that makes us blackfullas sick.

'It's no good for the old blackfulla ta live that way,' he reckons.

And he's probably right cos he aint been sick a day in his life.

Old Billy aint never married neither cos all the women he was ever with wanted to live in a house in town. They wanted him ta git a job too. But he wasn't havin any of that. He don't like bein back-chatted either, and he reckons women can't help doin that. 'Best ta leave em alone,' he says.

Anyway, one day we was fishin for yeller-belly with Uncle Billy. We was just sittin there real quiet when we hear these speedboats. They sounded like mosquitoes in the distance and then they got louder and louder and ya could hear fullas yellin and laughin.

Next thing ya know the boats are flyin past us at a hundred miles an hour, churnin the water up and frightenin the birds clean outta the trees.

Unc looks at us. 'By the fuckinjesus,' he says. 'Those fullas have got the dust flyin now.'

Me and Ant looks at one another. Ant goes, 'Ya not wrong, Unc.'

★

Nutha time we was sittin round the fire with Unc, drinkin big mugs of tea. It was really early in the mornin and the mist was still hangin over the river. We was all real quiet, like fullas are when they aint been awake for too long. So anyway, we was watchin the fire and next thing we see this bull ant start walkin up this big twig. He keeps goin. When he gits to the top, he stops for a second and then throws imself into the fire.

'Must have been jilted,' Unc reckons.

'Yeh.'

The show comes to town

Jackie White was the best truck driver around the back country. Never needed no help loadin or tarpin or tyin down the rig. Always delivered on time. Old Neville Jones reckoned he'd be fucked without Jackie drivin for him.

Never marryin or shackin up with anyone, Jackie was born, raised and still lived in the same house as old Mr and Mrs White, who died within a year of each other, leavin Jackie alone. Jackie wasn't too flash on makin friends or hangin out with people. Preferred the company of Yodel, the Jack Russell terrier who always rode up front in any rig or vehicle Jackie was drivin.

Jackie was long and skinny and had skin the colour of a well-polished cowboy boot. Always wore baggy blue jeans, a blue denim shirt hangin over the jeans, cowboy boots and a battered akubra pulled down over a long, crinkled face. Jackie looked like most drivers and workers out in the back country, but the thing that set Jackie apart was the eyes. Bluest ones you ever saw. Like the colour of the ocean Jackie never saw and never wanted to see.

Jackie probably woulda carried on just like always, drivin trucks with Yodel, drinkin seven-ounce beers and beatin everyone at pool in the pub. But then the travellin country show come ta town.

One of the fullas travellin with the show was me cousin, Big Kev Moolbong. Big Kev ran a toffee apple and fairy floss stand. He's a wiry little blackfulla, stands round five foot two, but Dad reckons he casts a big shadow. Big Kev is always neat as a pin in his polished cowboy boots with big Cuban heels, jeans always pressed and rolled up at the ankles, big flash belt buckle with a bucking bronco on it and shiny satin, fringed cowboy shirts.

Cousin Big Kev was the only child of Aunty Sippie and Uncle Benny Moolbong. They was show fullas from way back. They'd tried for years to have a baby, but no luck. Then when Aunty Sippie was forty-two and had given up, along comes Big Kev. Well they reckon you aint seen a spoilter kid. Not only Aunty Sippie and Uncle Bennie doted on im, but all the show fullas thought the sun shone outta him. He was brought up like a king. And the one thing he never was short on was confidence.

Big Kev loved going up to a woman and sayin, 'Big Kev Moolbong's the name. Pleased ta meet ya, got the meat ta please ya.'

He didn't do too good with the ladies though. But he didn't give a fuck, reckoned it was their loss. 'Cos they don't call me Big Kev on account me height.'

He'd say there was plenty more fish in the sea but, as Dad liked remindin him, he was 'livin in a fuckin desert'.

Anyway, this one time, me, Antman and Fleabag hooked up with im and his little mutt, Milton, when the show was in Antman's hometown for a week. When they was movin on, we took a job rouseaboutin with the show fullas cos we had nothin else to do at the time. We like movin round and it's good to git paid for it. Anyway, next town we blow into is Jackie White's. When we was finished settin up for the show to start next day, we wandered down to the only pub in town for a few beers and a game of pool.

Jackie White's sittin in there with just Yodel for company, so Flea and Milton who are mates from way back, go up to Yodel and start their introductions. They decide they like each other and go outside to continue the conversation. Anyway, Jackie turns to me, Antman and Big Kev and asks if we want a game of pool. Doubles. We reckon yeh and Big Kev offers to be Jackie's partner.

After a few hours of drinkin and gittin flogged at pool, me and Antman decide to head back to camp cos we got an early start in the mornin. We ask Big Kev if he's comin, but he's still yarnin with Jackie so he reckons he's gunna hang round for a while. We left im to it.

Next mornin he's settin his stand up happy as can be. Whistlin away as he gits everything ready for the day. All day he's nice as pie. Even give away a coupla free fairy flosses to some local kids. No one's ever seen im do that before. Apart from bein a grumpy bugger sometimes, he's still got the first quid he ever made.

That night, after the show shuts down, we ask Big

Kev if he wants to come for a beer, but he reckons no, he'll catch up with us the next day. We git down to the pub but there's no sign of Jackie or Yodel, so we ask the publican and he reckoned they took a rig out early that mornin and probably wouldn't be back till late.

Next night, the same thing. No Jackie, and no Big Kev. But on the third night, Big Kev says he'll see us down the pub.

So we're sittin there with a big heap of show fullas and locals when Big Kev struts in like a little bantam rooster. He's got Jackie White and Yodel in tow and the whole pub goes quiet cos Jackie White's wearin a fuckin dress!

It was a nice flowery one that come to just above the knee. It showed her legs, which were white as could be, and kinda funny lookin next to her brown and leathery face and hands. She wasn't wearin a hat and her hair was flattened down on her head. Big Kev was holdin her hand and grinnin from ear to ear as he and Jackie walked up to us.

'See there, tidda,' he says, 'ya old cuz made a woman out of er. They said it couldn't be done, but I done it!' he crowed.

Jackie sure didn't look too happy with all the attention and she specially wasn't happy with the dress. Kept havin to adjust the way she was sittin cos she was used to wearin trousers all the time. Everyone was askin her if she was givin up the rigs but before she could answer, Big Kev would butt in say she wouldn't have time for no truck drivin cos she'd be too busy lookin after him and all the kids they wuz gunna have.

Big Kev announced he was givin up the show life and settlin down with Jackie. Reckoned they might git hitched. He asked me and Ant to take over the toffee apple and fairy floss stand and we did for a time. Just until we could git someone else to run it, then we cruised back to the city. We was itchin for stayin still for a spell.

Bout three years later we went back out to Jackie's town to visit her and Big Kev. They had three kids. Two walkin and one a coupla months old. Seems like Jackie got pregnant straightaway, but her and Yodel stayed drivin rigs until two weeks before the first one was born. Two weeks after the birth, she left Big Kev and the kid and went back out on the road. Did the same with the next two as well.

Everyone reckoned it worked out real good. Big Kev kept a clean house and kids, and cooked real good tucker which fattened Jackie up a bit. He didn't seem too fussed about bein home while the missus went out ta work. He reckoned he'd spent his whole life on the road and said it sure was good to wake every day and know exactly where you was and whut you was gunna do for the day. He also reckoned bein an only kid weren't natural. That's why he wanted a whole bunch of em. He said im and Jackie was just like an old pair a emus in that Jackie had the kids and he looked after em.

No one ever saw Jackie in a dress again after that first night. When they got married she wore a slack suit and white cowboy hat.

We stayed with em for a coupla days on that last trip. Had a real good time and just before we was leavin, Jackie had ta take a rig over to Broken Hill and bring back a load. We was standin out the front, seein her off. Her and Yodel climbed into the truck and blew the horn nice and loud as they drove off up the red-dirt road. Big Kev's standin there with two kids and Milton beside im and nursin the little fulla. Antman looks at im.

'Yep,' he says, 'I gotta hand it to ya big fulla. You sure did make a woman outta Jackie White.'

Watchin a video with Aunty Joanie

One time me, Antman and Fleabag was round at his Aunty Joanie's house. We was watchin the *The Man from Snowy River* on the video.

We was watchin the scene where that fulla's ridin that horse flat chat down the mountain side. Over the rocks, round the trees, ridin him harder and faster as the decline of the mountain got steeper.

Aunty Joanie aint hardly drew a breath while all this is goin on. She gits real wrapped up in the movies and shows she watches and she don't mind huntin anyone outta the house if ya make too much noise while they're on.

Then as the fulla starts pushin that horse even harder, she grabs her hair and starts yellin at the TV. 'For Christ sake, ya rotten mongrel. Give that poor fuckin horse a spell.'

She got real wild with us when we started laughin.

Grandfather's medals

One time, not so long back, me, Antman and Fleabag was visitin me mum's mother, Nanna June. It was Nanna's eightieth birthday and we all went over for a big party. We had the deadliest time catchin up with all Ma's people.

Anyway, the next night we was all sittin round outside yarnin when Cousin Chookie turns up. She's Ma's first cousin. Her dad and Ma's dad were brothers. Ma and Chookie are more like sisters than cousins and spent the whole night of the party laughin over all the stuff they used to git up too when they was young fullas. Anyway, Chookie was real excited cos, as she put it, she had somethin real special to show everyone. She handed Nanna an old shoebox. Nanna opened it and pulled out a couple of rows of medals. They was Grandfather's war medals and he'd thrown em in the rubbish many years ago.

Nanna looked at the medals for a long while, turnin em over and over in her hands and then she started cryin. The tears was just rollin down her face. I aint ever seen

Nanna cry before. Ma reckoned she used to cry a lot when Grandfather was alive.

Grandfather died when I was real little, so I only remembered the fun Nanna, not the one Ma was always talking about. That Nanna was quiet and always workin, keepin the house like a new pin and makin sure supper was on the table at exactly the same time every night. The Nanna I knew played the squeezebox and mouth organ and loved to dance and go fishin. She was always givin cheek and cuddled ya just about every time ya walked past.

She finally dried her eyes and said to Chookie, 'Where did you git these, baby girl?'

'Mummy's had them all the time. When Uncle Georgie chucked em in the rubbish, she went and got em out and put em away. She reckoned one day you might want to have em back. She was gunna bring em round to you herself, but she thought that even if you were cranky at her for savin em all these years, you wouldn't yell at me. Ya won't, Aunt, will ya?'

Nanna looked up at her, the tears still runnin down her beautiful, old brown face. 'Of course I won't, Chookie.'

Ma took a good long look at the two rows of medals. Service medals, medals for bravery. All from Grandfather's service in World War Two, from when he had served in New Guinea and was a prisoner of the Japanese for two years.

Ma wasn't born when Grandfather went to war. That

happened a year after he got back. She'd never heard anyone talk about his time in the war, about bein a POW. She never knew he'd won medals. Grandfather never went to any ANZAC marches and always seemed to be a cold and distant man. Everyone was just a little bit scared of him, even though he never raised his voice or hit anyone. There was just this feelin that if he went off he wouldn't know how to stop.

Ma was real shocked that her dad had all those war medals and asked Nanna how come he'd thrown em away. How come no one ever talked about the fact he'd fought in the war, she wanted to know. And what happened to Grandfather when he was there?

Nanna cried for a while longer, then dried her eyes and started to tell us how the medals came to be thrown in the garbage.

'First thing, daught. It aint what happened to ya father when he was in the war. Not even bein a prisoner of war. It was what happened when he come home.

'Your father was one of the handsomest fullas you ever saw. A hard worker and real clever. He invented a little irrigation system so I wouldn't have ta cart water fom the river and he built us the best house out on the common with separate bedrooms and a nice bathroom outside. He played the guitar and accordion and sang all the time. We used ta sing and play together.

'We was real happy. Then the war come and even though blackfullas didn't have ta go, a lot of em from round here went. They reckoned it was their country, they had to keep it safe. Some of the fullas had to stay behind to look after the women and kids, cos we wasn't safe from a lot of the whitefullas. They used to like sneakin round our camp at night. If there wasn't some of our men there, I dunno what woulda happened. Gawd, I wish Georgie had been one of the ones to stay behind.

'When they came and told me he was in a prisoner of war camp, I nearly went mad with worry. I didn't think I'd ever see Georgie again. Ya know, in a way I never did. Not the one I knew anyway.

'When he come back he was as skinny as a rake and real quiet. Couldn't git boo outta im. Just sat inside all day starin at the wall. Didn't laugh anymore and didn't play his guitar anymore. That was okay cos I thought I could fatten him up again. And I reckoned if I give him enough time, maybe he would come round to bein the old Georgie again. I thought for sure when I got pregnant he would come round and for a while he did. But then things happened one after the other that just knocked the life and the love clean outta him.

'First he wants to go to the pub to celebrate and catch up with old mates he fought in the war with. He gits down the pub and they tell him he has ta go drink round the back, he can't go into the public bar. He went off his head. They reckon he started yellin bout fightin for this country, bout spendin two stinkin years as a prisoner of the Japanese and now he can't git a drink in a bloody pub in the town he wuz born in!

'When he come home I thought to gawd he'd take a

gun and go and blow everyone's head off down there. I thought he'd take it and shoot himself. But the saddest thing is, he just sat down in the corner and put his head in his hands and bawled his eyes out. I didn't know whut to do for him. I didn't know or understand whut he was goin through and he wuz cut off from the only fullas who did understand, cos of the colour of his skin.'

Nanna started cryin again and we told her she didn't have ta go on if she didn't want to. But she said she'd been carryin all this grief round for too long and it was time to bring it out in the open. She dried her eyes and went on.

'Next thing that happened wuz he needed to go and git a job to support me and the kids but there wuz no work in town so he decided to go shearin. Only trouble is he had to go and git a piece of paper to say he was good enough to go and git a job. We used to call em dog tags. That was the end for him. He reckoned they never asked him to produce a paper sayin he was fit ta die for his country. Anyway, we needed to eat so he went and applied for the paper and the day it arrived, he took his medals and chucked em in the bin.

'He never went on any ANZAC marches and he never talked about the war. He would turn off the television whenever there was a war picture on. He thought when he got back that he and his family would be treated as good as the whitefullas. He couldn't understand that we had to sit in special roped-off areas at the pictures. He hated that I couldn't try on dresses in the store. And it sure did break his heart that his mates never stuck up for him bout goin into pubs. I tried to say that maybe they was scared for themselves and their own families, but he wouldn't have it.'

Nanna looked at Ma and said, 'Your father died a broken man, daught.'

Ma was cryin now so I went over and put my arms around her. Dad was just sittin there lookin at the floor. He didn't know what to say. Chookie was upset cos she thought Nanna would be happy to have the medals back.

Finally Nanna said she was glad. She reckoned she went to rescue em later but they was gone. She was glad that they had been kept safe in the family all these years and told Chookie to tell her mother ta come round and have a yarn with her.

The next day we all got dressed up and went down to the park where there was a big plaque with the names of all the men who had served in World War Two. Grandfather's name was there, engraved in gold. Ma had walked past that plaque all her life and never knew her father's name was on it. Nanna placed her sad old hand on it as tears fell down her beautiful, soft brown face. She whispered something and stepped away, and one by one we all went up and said our silent peace to Grandfather's troubled soul.

When Ma stepped away she just said, 'I wish I'd known what he went through. Maybe I could have been a better daughter to him and maybe I could have taught you kids how to be better grandkids to him.'

Nanna gave the medals to Ma. Reckoned they were her legacy, so she took them home and polished em up and put them in pride of place on the mantlepiece. My brother says he wants to wear them in the local ANZAC march next year. Ma reckons she'll have to think real hard bout that.

Whitefulla dreamin

Me, Antman and Fleabag was fruit pickin down south when we run across a bunch a dreadlocked ferals in an old beat-up panel van. They was doin some pickin to git enough money to go up north to what they reckoned was gunna be a dreamin festival. They reckoned we should go along. They reckoned it'd be real 'trippy'.

Even though me and Ant is blackfullas, we aint ever been to a dreamin festival. Anyway, cos it was up north and we aint ever been up that way, we reckoned if we went, we could git ta meet all our bruthas and sistas from the coast and the mountains; git ta hear bout their mob and their ways. So we thought what the fuck, let's just cruise up there and check it out.

So when we finished up work we headed up that way. We weren't used to all those mountains, windin roads, all that thick forest. We both reckoned there'd be a lot of powerful spirits livin in there in the damp and the dark, so we only travelled during the day. We liked the ocean and the beaches and camped out on them for a few days. But cos we aint used to the ocean, we didn't swim out too far and Flea give it a miss altogether, which was funny cos he loves swimmin. Ant reckons it's cos he's a freshwater mutt that he didn't trust the ocean and never stopped barkin till we was outta the water and safe on the beach.

Anyway, we gits up to this little town. It was lousy with hippie and feral fullas. They was all headin out to the festival so we just followed em. There was camps everywhere and all kinds of em. Some was in trees, and there was teepees, tents, lean-tos, campervans, and some people just had swags on the ground, and some were campin in caves. They all had dreadlocks and dressed in cheesecloth and old tie-dyed shirts, t-shirts with Che and Mao on the front, ragged old trousers and skirts that twirled round the women's legs when they moved. Some had no clothes on at all. All their kids were dressed the same and had dirty faces. They was all gittin in touch with nature and livin on mung beans, home-made wine and yahndi. Ant reckoned a lot of em could afford to starve for a while cos they probably had trust funds and could rely on mummy and daddy to send money if they needed to.

There was fullas playin guitars and sitars and bongo drums and funny lookin Japanese flutes. Some were dancin to the music you could hear, some dancin to music only they could hear. There was some fullas just whirlin round and round in the same spot. Ant asked someone what they was doin and he said they was whirlin dervishes and followed some ancient religion from the Middle East.

There was all kinds of stalls sellin all kinds of shit. String bags, crystals, hand-made jewellery, painted rocks, clothes, hand-made flutes and other kinds of musical instruments. We walked round for a long time lookin at things, and listenin to the different bands. One thing for sure, there was no country music and sure as fuck there was no other blackfullas.

Ant said ta me, 'If this is supposed ta be a dreamin festival, where are all the fuckin blackfullas?'

While we was wanderin round the stalls tryin, in vain it turns out, ta find a food stall that sold tucker with meat in it, we come across a stall sellin didgeridoos, or yidakis as the fulla sellin em liked to call em. They was decorated with Koori symbols and dot paintins so Ant asked who painted em and who he was sellin em for. Proud as punch the fulla said that he made and painted em. Said he'd lived up in the Territory with 'real Yolngu people' and they adopted him into their tribe and give im a skin name and give im permission to make the yidakis and use their dreamin to decorate em. He asked me and Ant if we'd ever been to the Territory to meet 'real Yolngu people'. He told us it would be nice for us to know about our black side. He said he pitied us fullas who weren't full blood and what a shame it was that he probably knew more about Aboriginal people than we did. Me and Ant was dumbstruck at what he was sayin to us. He reckoned because he'd been adopted into the tribe he had what we didn't. His own dreamin place. Ant told him if he didn't shut his fuckin mouth he'd be back there before he knew it.

The fulla looked like he was gunna shit himself and he stammered, 'Hey, chill out man.'

Anyway, we decided to leave before things got ugly. It takes a lot to rile Antman. I don't remember im ever bein that pissed off before. Later he reckoned he was glad he didn't belt that fulla. He reckoned it wasn't worth it. I reckoned he was right.

Cos there was no other blackfullas around, everyone was fascinated with me and Ant and Fleabag. A lot aint ever met any of us before and they made a big show a comin over and talkin to us and sayin stuff like 'right on' or 'I hear ya' and callin us 'brutha' and 'sista' and makin sure we noticed the land rights stickers on their old Kombis and station wagons.

They played Archie Roach, Kev Carmody, Tiddas and No Fixed Address on their CD players.

Anyway, we started gittin sick of all the attention. We didn't feel like answerin any more questions bout whut it was like bein black. We was particularly sick of bein told we wasn't proper blackfullas too. More to the point we was sick of all this gammon whitefulla dreamin. We was just on for chillin and livin in different country for awhile. But all the mountains and the forests and sticky air and the drizzlin rain was different to anything we ever knew. We never felt dry. And we never did meet any other blackfullas at the festival.

So anyway, we'd had a gutful and was sittin in a

pub discussin our next move when this feral fulla, with dreadlocks down to his arse and wearin a Bob Marley t-shirt and carryin a big string bag full a shit, comes skippin over to our table.

He plonks himself down at our table and says, 'Hello Aboriginal people.'

We look at im and say, 'Hello Anglo man.'

He looks a bit upset about that. Ant reckoned later that he expected us to be able to see that, despite his white skin, he had a black soul. But he pulls himself together and says, 'So, I would be deeply honoured if you told me about your culture.'

I could hear the sigh come from the very bottom of Antman's guts as he said to the feral, 'Mate, ya gittin a bit personal, aint ya? Besides, me doctor aint got the results back from the lab yet.'

The feral gits up and moves away. Me, Antman and Fleabag head for the car and the back country. We drive all night. We aint afraid of the spirits in the damp, dark green country anymore.

The hundred-dollar bill

Dad and Hollywood worked together on the local council for years. Dad drove the council truck and Hollywood swept the gutters and emptied the bins on account he didn't have a truck licence.

Hollywood was a whitefulla who had an opinion on everything and reckoned he was always right whether he was or not. The blackfullas give im his name cos he loved sayin, 'Don't try and tell me what to do, old son. I'm the main actor in this fuckin show!'

He was tight as a fish's arse too. No one ever saw im shout a beer for anyone, and if he went to a party, he took along bottles of home brew that tasted like cat's piss. 'Twenty cents a bottle and ya can't tell the difference,' he liked to brag, before drinkin everyone else's good grog. His glass was always half full if it wuz his shout and half empty when it wuz yours.

He lived at home with his parents and paid no rent. His mum cooked, cleaned and did his laundry. He turned up shinin like a new pin everyday. He idolised his dad and they did everything together, like makin the home brew and playin golf on Saturdays, rain or shine.

He sort of had a girlfriend. She was one of the council supervisors. Used to come to town every six weeks and they'd go to the club for Chinese. Always split the bill right down the middle and then they'd go for a little drive.

Anyway, one mornin Dad comes into the depot and Hollywood's perched up behind the wheel of the council truck with a big grin on his face and lookin like he'd just won first prize in the lottery. He leans out and says to Dad, 'Take a little spell from drivin today, old fulla. I got me truck licence yesterday.'

It sure did surprise Dad cos he didn't even know he was goin for it. Later Hollywood told im he'd found out they paid more if you could drive the truck. He'd never been known to pass up anything that fattened his wallet. Dad reckoned his supervisor girlfriend put im up to it. Told im there wuz an extra quid in it.

Dad wasn't real keen on the idea of anyone else doin the drivin cos he wasn't too fond of wearin out the soles on his council boots. But he thought he'd beat the bastard into work the next day so he let im go this time.

So next morning, Dad got into work ten minutes early only to find Hollywood perched up in the driver's seat, chirpy as can be. The next day he made it in twenty minutes early. Same thing. It didn't matter what time Dad got in, there was old Hollywood sittin up there, leanin over the steerin wheel, waitin to git started.

Dad reckoned that bastard must sneak back at night and fuckin sleep in the truck.

This went on for a coupla months, till one mornin, they're drivin along and Dad switches on the wireless to listen to the John Laws show. Only thing is, Hollywood's got it on another station. Now Dad's pretty easy goin. He don't git upset about too much in life, but there's three things in life where you don't argue with him and that's his beer (Melbourne Bitter long necks), the ABC news at night and Lawsie on the wireless in the mornin. Dad's been a fan for years. He's rung im up a few times and been sent bottles of Wild Turkey, CDs, a copy of his book of poems and one of his most treasured possessions, a John Laws clock.

So Dad goes to switch it over and Hollywood starts bungin on bout how he hated Lawsie and wanted to listen to somethin else. So Dad says he wasn't arguin with im, it was Lawsie or nothin. Hollywood looked im straight in the eye.

'I didn't make the rules, Roy. If I remember rightly it was you who said whoever controls the steering wheel, controls the wireless dial. If I'm not mistaken, I'm the one behind the wheel.'

Well Dad reckons that bony-arsed little mongrel was lucky to be alive cos he reckons he aint ever wanted to wring someone's neck as much as Hollywood's that day. But Dad cops it and sits there fumin and thinkin bout good places to bury a body while Hollywood whistles along to the 'Baby Elephant Walk' and 'The Little Spanish Flea'.

That night me, Antman and Fleabag are round at Uncle Ronnie's place, chillin out with im and Flash and Myrtle. We hear Dad bungin on next door and then Ma tellin im ta piss off and ta come back when he's woken up to himself.

So then Dad comes stormin into Uncle Ronnie's and starts goin on bout Hollywood. He's worked himself up into a real state but Unc tells him to settle down and hands him a long neck. After Dad quietens down Unc tells im he's gotta beat that little arsehole at his own game. He points over to Myrtle who's havin a nap under a tree and reminds im that he was always tellin im he was weak as piss, but now he was carryin on the same way. Dad reckoned Unc was right. Hollywood had him carryin on like a real clown. He had to bring a bit of blackfulla cunnin to the proceedins.

Anyway, the next day Dad's sweepin the footpath and he calls up to Hollywood. 'Come and have a look at what I found. Ya not gunna bloody believe it!'

So Hollywood hops outta the truck and saunters over. Dad shows im a crisp $100 note. Hollywood's eyes bug out and he starts tremblin at the sight of that lovely lookin green bill.

'Where'd ya git that, Roy?' he asks, his voice all choked up.

'It was right here in the gutter. I wuz sweepin away and I looked down and there the fuckin thing wuz. Some poor bastard's gunna be cranky when he finds that missin. Couldn't come at a better time though, aye? Two days before pay day! I'd give ya half, old mate, but I know how ya feel about the old finders keepers bit.'

Hollywood goes real pale and tells Dad he'll see im back in the truck. Dad said he hardly opened his mouth for the rest of the day and when they finished work he just climbed down from the wheel and got in his ute and pissed off without sayin a word of goodbye. Dad reckoned Hollywood wouldn't have slept much that night.

The next mornin Dad goes into work bright and early but the shed's still locked up. He goes in and makes himself a cuppa and waits for Hollywood. He turns up about half an hour later, big, dark circles under his beady eyes. He apologises for bein late, reckoned he wuz buggered if he could sleep last night.

'Ya git that on the big jobs,' Dad says, and says they better git to work.

He starts walkin over to the passenger side but Hollywood chucks im the keys.

'You drive today, Roy. Take a load of your feet. I'll sweep the gutters.'

'You sure?' asks Dad.

'Yeh, mate. I've been hoggin the driver's seat for too long.'

'Whatever ya reckons a fair thing, old mate,' says Dad as he fairly floats into the driver's seat. First thing he does is switch the wireless back to Lawsie.

That night Dad gives Uncle Ronnie back his $100 bill. We all sat round, polished off a slab a beer and laughed our guts out for hours. Ma was happy too. She'd had a gutful of Dad comin home moanin all the time.

Hollywood aint driven that truck since and people reckon the old town's got the cleanest gutters in the whole country.

Mothballs

Aunty Sugar is an old devil. She likes makin people shame, specially young fullas. I remember when I first took Antman out ta meet her. Aunt's got a big old tea chest she calls her glory box. It's full a sheets and towels, pillowcases, tablecloths, pots and pans, cups and saucers. Her ma and dad started it for her when she was a little kid. They wanted her to have all the things they didn't when she finally grew up and married. The thing is Aunty Sugar never did git married. She was thirty-six before they stopped buyin her stuff.

Aunty Sugar just wasn't one for the lads. She liked muckin round with em, havin a drink and laugh, but she reckoned she never met one that pushed any of her buttons. She worked all her life as a shearers' cook and earned a lot of money and owned a little house just outside town. She decked out the place with a lotta stuff from the glory box, but there was so much more in there she wouldn't ever use. So on birthdays, all her nieces, if they was around, got ta go and pick somethin out of all the things that was left as a present.

Aunty never had any romance as far as anyone can tell. Ma reckons a nurse come to work at the hospital one time and her and Aunt spent a lot a time together. Reckoned they was real sweet on each other. But Ma reckoned Sugar just wasn't able to come ta terms with what she was feelin, so the nurse left town. Ma reckoned that nurse cried like her heart was breakin when she got on the train and went back to the city. No one saw Aunty Sugar for a long while after that. Ma reckoned she told her she was a fuckin fool for lettin that chance for a bit of love and happiness git away. Aunt looked at her like she didn't know what she was talkin bout. But ya can't fool Ma. Not ever.

Anyway, Aunty Sugar got over it all and seemed content livin in her little house, with her bantam roosters and three dogs and cookin for the shearin teams.

But like I said, she was a devil. Anyway, this time I was out home for my birthday and she sent Dad up to fetch me. So me, Antman and Fleabag went out to her place. She was out the back in the yard collectin some eggs from her chooks when we turned up. She's got everything out there. A veggie patch, grapevines, fruit trees. She's always sendin eggs and fruit to relations. She turns to us with a box of eggs and tells us to take em home to Ma and Dad.

She gives me a big kiss and hug for me birthday and says, 'You know where the glory box is, baby girl. Go and pick somethin out for your present.' So I goes in and all the stuff's wrapped in tissue paper and packed up nice and neat and there's mothballs scattered all around. The smell of camphor is overpowerin.

Ant aint ever smelt it before so when Aunty comes in he asks her what the smell is and Aunty Sugar tells him, 'It's mothballs, boy. Aint you ever seen mothballs?'

'Course I have,' reckons Ant. 'I just forgot what they smelt like.'

'So you've not only seen mothballs, you've smelt em too! Well tell me, boy, how'd ya git their little legs open?'

I aint ever seen a blackfulla go red till that day. Aunty Sugar roared with laughter.

She looks over at me and starts wipin her eyes with her hanky and says, 'It's an old one but a good one eh, daught?'

'Sure is, Aunt,' I reckoned. I had ta borrow a hanky meself.

Aunty Sugar don't mind shamin whitefullas either. I remember one time we was all at a weddin. It was one of her nephews and he was marryin a white girl. Her brother told her she could go but reckoned she wasn't allowed to muck up and drink too much and give cheek. She promised she'd behave. 'On my dyin oath, brother,' she reckoned.

So she turns up and she's all dolled up and bein nice as pie. She's sittin with me and Ma, Dad and Antman and tryin her level best not ta fuck up. She was goin real good too. We nearly got to the end of the night and Aunt hadn't insulted anyone, and as much as it was killin her cos it was free, she was goin real easy on the grog.

Anyway, right towards the end of the reception one of the old white women from the bride's family comes over to our table for a yarn. She'd been loosenin up a bottle of gin and had a bit of the old wobbly boot on. She plonked herself down next to Aunt and started makin small talk. Aunt was nice as pie answerin all the lady's questions and keepin a 'civil tongue in her head' just like Uncle wanted her too. The lady told Aunt how the family had been worried about Gretchen marryin an Aboriginal at first, but he's turned out to be such a lovely boy. 'My gosh,' she said, 'if you closed your eyes you would think you were talking to a white man when you're talking to Dane.'

Aunty grit her teeth and says, 'Yeh, I don't know how, but sometime we fluke a good one.'

'You certainly do,' said the lady takin another swig from her gin.

Then the lady started complimentin Aunt on her good looks and her nice skin and Aunt's lappin it up. Then she asks Aunt how old she is and Aunt tells hers she's sixty-five.

The old lady looks surprised. 'Sixty-five?' she says. 'How unusual. I didn't think you Aboriginal people lived that long. I mean with all the violence and the alcohol and the drugs and whatnot.'

'Well,' says Aunt, takin a big slug of beer and fixin her large black eyes on the lady. 'Well, my dear,' she says in a really flash voice. 'I only sniff unleaded petrol.'

Even though Uncle told us to keep an eye on Aunt and

chip her if she mucked up, we couldn't help ourselves. The whole table just busted out laughin.

The old white lady looked at Aunt in a confused sort of way. Then when she at last realised she was gittin the piss taken she got up and staggered off. Unc saw the commotion and come stormin over. When we told im what happened he started laughin too. He went and got Aunt a fresh beer. A whole jug all to herself.

The purebred pedigree

Boris is Antman's best mate. They been mates since they was kids. Boris arrived at the same school as Ant one day. He was a lanky, skinny kid who could hardly speak English. All the kids called him a greasy wog and used to flog im up all the time. Till one day Antman come across a coupla kids pickin on im and towelled em up. Ant told Boris he had to toughen up a bit, learn ta stick up for himself.

He took im round to his place and Ant's dad give Boris boxin lessons and everyone else taught him how to speak like an Aussie. Trouble is, it was Aussie blackfulla style. Bonnie loves tellin the story bout the first time she took Boris home. Him and his family had spent their first year in Australia in a migrant camp and then they moved into a little three-bedroom fibro Commission house. So he was real impressed when he sees Bonnie's place. A great big, four-bedroom, blonde-brick veneer with a patio and above-ground swimmin pool out the back. Bonnie reckons his eyes bugged out. 'By the fuckin bejesus,' he said, 'this sure is a flash lookin camp. You fullas must have a heap a wulung ta live in a camp like this.'

He confuses people by askin where the jillawa is when he wants to go to the toilet and callin dogs mirrigarns.

Anyway, him and Ant become the best of friends, always together. When Ant got sick and lost all his hair, Boris got his shaved off and got his ma to make em both flash bandanas. He didn't grow his hair back till Ant's did.

Ant calls Boris the Battered Slav, or BS for short, and he loves it. He's grown into a big bear of a man, with long black hair, wild hazel eyes and the biggest laugh you ever heard. When Ant took Boris out to meet his people, he scared the life outta all those blackfullas, but now they love im. They specially love teachin him the lingo. Ant loves it when they git back ta town and there's Boris confusin everyone with these strange black words. One of his favourites is boongalungs, which is our lingo for balls. He loves goin up ta whitefullas and askin em how their boongalungs are. Him and Ant git the biggest laugh when they say, 'Good thanks, mate. Real good.'

Boris got married real young cos his girl Bonnie got pregnant. Ant was his best man. When Boris had his two kids, Ant was godfather. Whenever Bonnie kicked Boris out (which was a lot) he come and stayed with Ant.

Every week durin footy season me, Antman and Fleabag went over to his place to watch the game on his big screen. Anyway this day we was standin at his front door when next thing we hear was Bonnie. 'Get your fat fuckin Croat arse outta my house. And take that lazy mongrel with ya,' she was screamin, hurlin a garbage bag of clothes at Boris.

It landed on his big guts, upsetting the mull bowl resting on it and scatterin the contents over Boris and his beloved blue heeler Trev, causing the dog to sneeze violently. Trev was the apple of Boris' eye. Besides Antman and Bonnie, and his two boys, there was no one or nothin that Boris loved more than Trev. He bought him down the pub for twenty dollars, with the papers included, and the two of em have been inseparable ever since.

'Now look what ya done,' yelled Boris. 'Ya made Trev sneeze. And another fuckin thing, if I've told ya once, I've told ya a thousand fuckin times, Trev might be lazy, he might be an arsehole, but he's no fuckin mongrel. He's a purebred, pedigree blue heeler with the papers to prove it.'

Bonnie was a bit shocked at Boris yellin back at her. He never got upset bout anythin, but one thing he wouldn't put up with was anyone calling Trev a mongrel. He had Trev's pedigree papers framed and in pride of place on the mantelpiece, something that really pissed off Bonnie.

'Just get yourself and that useless mongrel outta here. Now!' she snarled, after recovering from her initial shock.

Boris knew there was no use pleading his case. He also knew it was well deserved and a long time coming. Bonnie just looked at us and turned round and went into her room. Boris asked if he and Trev could come and camp with us for a coupla days and we said okay. So he dusted the mull residue off his Guns N' Roses t-shirt, gathered up his clothes, bong, mull bowl, bean bag, esky, framed pedigree papers, and Trev with his black and white striped kapok hairball of a cushion in his mouth, and headed out the door to his 1980 black Holden ute. He told us he'd see us round home. The only sound louder than the roar of the V8 engine was the slammin of doors and the cursin of Bonnie.

About twenty minutes later he pulled up at our place.

'So she finally had a gutful, eh?' said Antman, twisting the lid off a chilled stubby.

'Fuckin moll,' muttered Boris.

'Aye, aye mate. Enough of that. Bonnie is your wife, the mother of your kids. She's a really good sheila too. I dunno how she's put up with you all these years.'

'Ya right as usual, mate.'

'Anyway,' said Ant, 'you know where the room is. Sling us a couple of bob. I'll duck down the bottlo and grab a slab. Reckon we're gunna need it.'

Boris reached into his jeans pocket, fished out a hundred-dollar note and handed it to Ant.

'Make it two and packet of tobacco while ya at it, old son.'

'No worries,' said Ant.

Boris pulled up a deck chair and helped himself to a stubbie. Trev plopped his pillow down beside him and assumed the nap position. He'd pretty well spent the whole of his five years in the nap position. He was about as animated as a painting on velvet was Trev. Fleabag couldn't figure Trev out. He didn't understand how a dog wouldn't play, and chase stuff and dig things up. All his other mates, Humbug, Yodel, Flash, Harry and mutts from all over the place could be relied on for a bit of fun and games, but not Trev.

Flea tried all sorts of things. Runnin at im and nippin im so he'd chase im. But all Trev would do was lick his boongalungs and go back ta sleep. One time he went and sat on Trev's cushion, but Trev just ambled over and grabbed it by his teeth and pulled it out from under Flea. He give up after that and just sits doin nothin when Trev's around. It suits Boris though cos he can't be arsed takin him for walks or teachin him tricks. Trev's sole job is to accompany Boris on his fixed daily routine of goin to work at the local park where he works with the maintenance crew, then on to the pub, then home for a couple more beers, some bongs, dinner and bed. On weekends he goes to the pub to watch footy or cricket, then we and a few other mates go to his place for the replay and for joints and beers afterwards. Even though Bonnie was always rowin with im about it, the routine rarely changed.

Anyway, after Antman come back from the bottlo, he sat down, opened a beer for himself and passed one to me and Boris. 'So what happened, mate?' he asked. 'She's kicked you out before, but this looks serious. You've never brought the bean bag and the dog's papers before.'

'Well,' he replied, 'she nags me for fuckin weeks to

go see that bloody Irish dancin show at the rissole with her. I say you don't need me to go. But oh no! She gives me the old "you never take me anywhere" routine so I do the right thing. So we get there and she gits the shits and reckons I'm drinkin too much. Then she accuses me of pervin on her friends and ignorin her. I mean for fuck sake, what's a bloke to do? And then we git home and she bungs on for a doorie. I said, "Darl, you know he's useless after a few drinks, just give him till mornin. He'll rear up again." But no, she starts crying, sayin I don't find her desirable anymore. Fuckin desirable! Where do they come up with this shit?

'Anyway, she still had the shits this mornin and boots me out, but to tell ya the truth I've had a gutful. I turned a blind eye while she was muckin round with Steve from the bottlo.'

'Yeh, mate. But fair go,' reckoned Ant. 'You were getting free piss and she was leaving you alone.'

'True,' replied Boris. 'I agree there were certain advantages for me, but that's not the point. Anyway, what I was goin to say was, I didn't go down to the pub and bung on with em or nothin. I let em have their way. I work, give her anything she wants and she's still not happy. Okay, I can put up with that, but when she starts bringin Trev into the equation, starts callin him a fuckin mongrel, then it's time to pull the pin.'

'Yeh, there's no need to bring Trev into it,' said Antman, packing a cone and waving away a blowfly at the same time.

The blowie then decided to bother Boris. He turned to Antman.

'You got any fly spray or one of them swatters, mate? This fuckin thing's really givin me the shits.'

'Leave her alone,' said Ant, firing up the bong. 'She's not doing any harm.'

'Mate, it's annoyin. And how do know it's a she?'

Antman finished his cone and after turning several shades of purple and red, coughin and splutterin like an old wino, handed the device to Boris and wheezed, 'It lays eggs, idiot. She needs a warm, smelly place for those maggots and I suppose she thought your arse was a good a place as any.'

'I should be flattered then,' said Boris, packing his own cone.

'Look, they serve a purpose, BS. They're like cleaners, they lay their eggs in carcasses, shit, anything left lying round and rotting. They suck up all the nutrients and what's left is shit you can sweep up, or clean bones rather than sloppy stuff and rotting bodies we weak-gutted humans can't handle. If we didn't have things like that, mate, we'd all be fucked. Besides, she's probably got little tackers waiting for her at home. What happens when she doesn't front cos you can't handle her buzzin around.'

'I reckon you're just too lazy to get the fly spray, mate. But you've got a point,' replied Boris, giving Trey a tummy tickle and causing the dog to play a pretty mean air guitar version of 'Highway to Hell' with his back legs.

'Anyway, let her live to fly and spread disease and maggots another day.'

'Glad to see your broken heart has not stripped you of your humanity,' Ant reckons.

So we were all nicely stoned and, with an esky full of coldies, we settled into a happy silence. Then, to everyone's amazement, Trev decided to get up from his cushion. Lumberin over to his fully stocked food and water bowls, he nibbled on a couple of doggy biscuits, took a long, noisy drink, gave himself a good shake and, clearly exhausted, headed back to the comfort of his cushion.

The blowie was still hoverin around making random swoops on Boris who by now was well beyond caring. Trev stood as Boris gave him a tickle behind the ears. As he was about to collapse on his cushion the blowie buzzed by, so Trev quickly snapped it into his mouth. After some teeth gnashin and violent head tossin, the blowie was gone and Trev once again assumed the nap position.

Antman just looked at the dog.

'Fair dinkum, Trev. Sometimes you're not worth feeding, ya fuckin mongrel.'

Suddenly upright, Boris turned to Antman and growled, 'Watch it, mate. He's no fuckin' mongrel.'

'Yeh, yeh, I know. He's a purebred, pedigree blue heeler with the fuckin papers to prove it.'

'And don't you fuckin forget it,' said Boris, firing up another cone.

Me, Antman and Fleabag hook up

I'm the first born of Ma and Dad and come into this world a healthy seven and a half pound baby. I stayed that way for the first coupla years of me life, living with Ma and Dad out in the desert country.

Then Ma went to hospital to have my brother. She left me laughing, happy and healthy. Five days later she returned to me lying in a cot, barely able to breathe. She tried to make me stand. I collapsed. She took me in her arms and ran the five miles into town. That was the beginning of me nightmare. I was real sick. The doctors flew me to a hospital for children in the city and ...

I stayed there for a few years. When I was well enough, I was sent to a convalescent home to learn to walk again, to be rehabilitated. For the next three years, from the onset of the illness to me eventual reunion with me family, I did not once see another blackfulla, let alone even see another Aboriginal face.

When you're a little fulla you see your reflection in those around you. And all the faces that surrounded me were white. They wore stiff, starched uniforms, everything was clean, antiseptic, and everything was ordered. I lived in a safe, clean, little white world.

Then came the day that me and Ma and Dad will never forget. It started out like any other day – up early, bathed, fed. The only thing different I was dressed in a brand new pinafore, new top, shoes, socks and me hair was tied in ribbons. I was thinkin I was goin for a day out with Linda the cook. Anyway, I was excited about the new clothes. I felt like a princess. Then I was told I was going to meet some special people and they were taking me on a long journey.

'But they'll bring me home, won't they?' I said.

They were evasive. 'Maybe one day. For a visit.'

'Are they taking me away forever and ever? They can't do that, can they?'

I saw tears in the nursing sister's eyes. I was confused and started to feel frightened.

Then I was taken into the visitors' room where before me stood two aliens from another world. It was Ma and Dad.

'This is your mummy and daddy,' said the sister as she passed me to the strange dark lady.

I remember screamin. 'She's not Mummy, he's not Daddy. They're black.'

Tears streamed down their faces. I reckon it woulda hurt em real bad. I was handed over to these two dark-skinned and cryin strangers, screamin in terror. No one give me a chance to git ta know these people. After all these years they just handed me to em. Just like that.

Ma and Dad carried me, still screaming, into a bustling, noisy, crowded railway station, desperately tryin to ignore the suspicious stares of the strangers around em. All their soothin and strokin did no good. I just kept right on cryin, even when we got into the carriage at Central. Suddenly, the train began to move and soon we were passin through suburbs and then countryside. I started gittin curious.

'Where are we goin? Is that a real cow? Are you really my mummy and daddy?'

'We're goin home now, me baby,' said the dark-skinned lady.

Now that I wasn't strugglin, she seemed so soft. Her eyes were big and brown but full of tears.

'You mean back to the ward?'

'No, baby girl, back to your real home. You got a baby brother and sister. They're called Buddy and Lulla. Home to your grandma and grandpa.'

I started to relax. Daddy was makin funny faces at me and pointing out the animals. The trip seemed to take forever, but this kind and gentle woman held me all the way. When I become sleepy, I nestled my head in her breasts, and her blouse was damp from both our tears. I went to sleep.

The next morning, the train pulled up at a small railway station, smack dab in the middle of a vast red desert. There were no big trees, just little saltbush ones. A radio was blarin from the station office, breakin the eerie silence as we stepped off the train.

I was used to the big houses and leafy surrounds of the North Shore. These people I had started to trust really were aliens. They had taken me to Mars.

Daddy took me from Mum and hoisted me on his shoulders. We started walking cross the vast expanse of red earth and strange little trees. We saw some emus and a kangaroo. A big yellow lizard ran in front of us. It was so hot. We seemed to walk for miles and then I could hear the sound of laughter. Someone was strummin a guitar and singin. We walked into a clearin, where in a circle were huts made from scrap, tents and a coupla caravans. There was dogs and kids everywhere and people all the same colour as the people who had brought me here.

It sure did come as a surprise when I finally looked into a mirror and realised I was the same colour as them.

These people surrounded me. An old man with silver hair, a dark face and twinkling eyes took me from Ma's arms and held me. 'Me little bubby's home at last,' he whispered.

I was passed from grandparents, to aunts and uncles, investigated by cousins and introduced to two scrawny little black kids who they said was my brother and sister.

We walked towards a large tent. Dad was carryin me. I looked at the tent, and in me childish innocence asked, 'Daddy, who owns this cubby house?'

He didn't answer; just handed me to Mum.

Two hours later he came back with a large blue caravan. He just looked at Ma and said, 'Can't expect her to live in a tent, not after what she's been livin' in.'

He still talks about that day. His pride was hurt. I was just as alien to them as they were to me. He built me a tiny little toilet of my own, with pink cabbage roses cut from a women's magazine pasted on the side.

I soon adapted, and started to forget about the hospital, forget about the convalescent home. I came to love my family.

We moved to another town with a river. Me dad bought a block of land and started work on building roads.

But my spells in hospital were far from over. For the next ten years, twice yearly I was taken kicking and screaming from Ma's arms to Sydney for further treatment. And each time having to undergo a mind transformation in order to cope with a changin two-toned world.

Finally, when I was thirteen, I had a coupla operations to put things right. I was put through eighteen painful months more of separation from me family who were too poor and had too many other kids to look after to be able to visit me. Once again I went home a stranger. It was supposed ta be home for good this time but I couldn't settle and a few years later I left again.

For a long time I lived in two worlds. One white, one black, and never really fitting into either. I went home often for Christmas, Easter, but family reminiscences left me out. I hadn't been there. Me brothers and sisters didn't seem to understand that I never wanted to be away when I was a kid.

I hardly knew the family, let alone my culture. All those years I drifted from one world to another, part of me missing.

I drank too much, probably, and could never bear to be in a job longer than six months. Anyone who tried to get too close was pushed away. It was just too hard. It was funny too. Cos even when I was in the arms of other fullas, some that I even really liked, my soul felt lonely. My skin felt lonely.

Then Antman come along.

I met him one night when I was feelin real down. Flat broke and busted on an off pay week – or as we blackfullas call it 'bumpers and buses week'. Pay week's always called 'taxi and tailor-mades week'.

Anyway, I was sittin out the front of home drinkin tea and smokin rollies when me cuz Neilly Boy come cruisin up. He reckoned, 'C'mon sista girl, got a pocket full a wulung. Git yaself styled up and we'll go to the club for Koorioke.'

Next thing ya know, we sail into the club and sit ourselves down at a table with a bunch a sistas and a coupla brothers who want to be sistas, puffin up and drinkin top shelf.

Next thing the Koorioke starts and we git a mob of blackfullas gittin up to have a sing. We hear 'Paper Roses', 'Stand by Your Man', 'Please Release Me' and 'Send Me the Pillow that You Dream On'. Everyone yells and cheers for all the singers cos they don't want any of em, even if they're woefuls, to feel shame.

Then next thing, this fulla gits up and starts singin 'Heard It Through the Grapevine' and everyone shuts up and starts lookin and listenin. I remember seein him and the rest of the room just disappearin. I could only see him; I could only hear him.

It aint that he was the best lookin fulla I ever saw, it was just that it felt like I was seein the lights of home for the first time. Next thing ya know, he's lookin right back at me while he's singin and when he finishes he comes straight over and introduces himself. That was it. I went home with him that night. We talked all night bout all kinds of things.

Turns out Antman had been crook when he was little fulla too. Spent a long time away from his family, just like me. We loved the same things – readin books, listenin to music, dogs, Slim Dusty, bein outside.

And before too long, we loved each other. Two days later he drove round to the house I'd been livin in and I packed a suitcase, grabbed my guitar and we aint been apart since.

It wasn't easy the first year. We was both used to bein on our own, doin what we pleased. We kept pullin each other in different directions.

One night, after I had too much drink, we had a terrible fight. The next day I was feelin sorry, feelin shame, askin him to forgive me.

He looked at me and said, 'I bet you've done this a

thousand times. Always asking for forgiveness, always thinking it's your fault. You don't think you're worthy of love. You don't know yourself. I gotta take you home, girl. Back to your people, your country. It won't be easy but you'll never find peace until you stop runnin.'

For the first time I listened to what someone else had to say. Finally someone was makin sense.

The next week we packed up the car and he took me back to the red dirt. Back to family, country and culture.

We lived for the next coupla years with my mob. We listened to the stories of our old people, learnt our language. I discovered my blackness. It wasn't easy. Strangely enough, while I was feeling sorry for myself because of my sickness and enforced separation, turns out the rest of the kids thought I had lived a privileged life.

One night me, Antman, Ma, Dad and me brothers and sisters had a few beers and we all started to talk about that day when they picked me up from the hospital. Ma told me how it tore her heart out to hear me say she couldn't be me mother. Dad told me how small he felt when I asked who lived in the cubby house that up until then had been their home. They told me how they suffered each time I went away. My brothers and sisters told me that they thought I lived a life of glamour; that I had it easy, that I had deserted them. They said they understood now that it was not my choice. Everyone told me how they wanted to protect me, wrap me in cotton wool, but they loved me enough not to.

Suddenly we were all crying. They were tears for what we had lost and tears for what we had gained. They were the warm salty tears of healing, and once again I lay my head on Ma's breast. Once again her blouse was damp from our intermingled tears.

After that night, me and Antman reckoned it was time to go back to the city for a spell. Just before we were about to leave one of me sisters come by with a little bundle of pure-white fluff. Lulla reckoned they couldn't find im a home cos he had a gammy leg from birth. She reckoned we needed him and he needed us. Antman took im from her and give im a big cuddle and said, 'Welcome home, ya little fleabag.'

And that was that. The next day he sat in the front seat between the two of us and he's been ridin there ever since. He's the greatest little mutt ever. He's cheeky and smart and he don't worry bout his gammy leg, just runs with the rest of the pack. All the blackfullas love im ta bits, specially the old fullas who fuss over im and tell us off if they reckon we aint lookin after im. Lulla was right, we sure did need that little fulla. Still do.

Fleabag's our kid. Antman can't have kids on account he had ta have chemotherapy when he was young and my sickness meant I couldn't have any either. I suppose we three was just meant to hook up.

A few months after we got Flea, we was all lyin in bed. It was early mornin, just before the sun come up. Antman was asleep with his arm across my belly and Fleabag's usin my leg for a pillow.

I suddenly felt all the loneliness leave me, finally makin room for all the good things in life, like family, laughin, travellin and, best of all, love.

Suddenly I felt all together. There was no more lonely soul, no more lonely skin.

Livin on the moon

One night me, Antman and Fleabag was havin a cuppa with Granny Edie and her oldest daughter Aunty Essie. Gran's ninety years old and Aunty Essie is seventy. Anyway, we was sittin out the front of their camp, sippin on enamel mugs of sweet, milky tea, eatin biscuits and lookin up at the sky. It was covered with a big heap of stars and there was a great big, old yellow moon sittin right in the middle of em.

'Ya know what, Mummy?' Essie starts.

'What, daught?' says Gran, dunkin her scotch finger in her tea and handin half ta Fleabag.

'Sometimes everything just gits ta me and I feel like gittin a great big ladder and climbin up and just livin on that moon.'

Granny finishes chewin on her half of the biscuit and looks up. 'Yeh, daught. I'll come with ya. I reckon it'd be nice up there.'

The drought breaks

Me little nephew Bunty was born in the middle of a long drought. There wasn't a drop of rain that fell in his first three years of life. All he knew was sunshine, heat and red dust.

Anyway, a few days after he turned three, he was playin outside when the drought broke. First the rain started in big heavy drops and Bunty looks up and wonders where the water's comin from. Then the rain starts comin down harder. Next thing ya know the sky's wailin.

Bunty starts to panic, and then he starts screamin and runnin round like a decapitated chook while he tries to wipe the giant drops of rain from his arms and head. Me sister and brother-in-law run outside ta see what's got into im.

Finally they realise the little fulla aint never seen rain before. He don't know what the fuck is goin on.

To make matters worse, all the dogs start barkin and howlin and Bunty is in such a state he's almost stopped breathin. Me sister and her husband start to panic as well. Then Ant goes runnin over, picks up Bunty, looks around and sees just what's needed to sort the situation. He belts over to the only spot not touched by rain and rolls Bunty in the dust. He calms down right away.

Me sister was real grateful and wondered why she never thought of doin that. We all had ta sit down and tell the little fulla bout rain and that it wasn't gunna hurt im.

We all prayed there was no thunder and lightin comin.

Aunty Tibby

One summer, after me, Antman and Fleabag finished a few weeks' fruit pickin, we decided to head home the long way, through river country, then out home to see my mob. We had a pocket full of wulung to spend and was in no hurry to git back to the city.

Anyway, the second day, we wuz chillin out by the river. Ant and Flea was fuck arsin round in the river and I was makin damper to go with the yeller-belly we caught. We had the fire right down to the ashes, just right for cookin, when a ute pulled up on the bank with a wiry little blackfulla with dreadlocks in it.

Ant and Flea saw im and come outta the river, Flea shakin himself as he walked out. I got up and we all walked over to the car and asked the fulla what he wanted and he says he heard there was a Wongaibon woman in town. I told im it was me.

So he gits out and says, 'Pleased ta meet ya, sis. Me name's Lennie Boy. Anyway, me Granny Tibby got wind you was in town and wants ya to come up to the hospital to meet her. She's old and sick and she aint got long to go, but she reckons it's real important she talks to ya.'

I asked im when visitin hours was and he reckoned anytime so I told im I'd go up in a coupla hours. Ant asked im if he wanted a feed or a cuppa but he reckoned no and told us to ask for Aunty Tibby at the hospital and he'd catch up with us later.

After our feed, we got cleaned up and headed to the hospital. It was a small hospital, really old and sittin on the banks of the river. Lots of big old trees and flowers and a few blackfullas sittin outside in the sun yarnin while they waited ta see the Flyin Doctor. Everyone nodded at us and one old fulla asked if we was the Wongaibon mob come to see Tibby. We reckoned yeh and asked if Flea could sit with em till we come back.

The old fulla reckoned Tibby had a room out the back on the garden and Flea could sit there. He told us he'd fetch im round in a coupla minutes. Flea had no problem with that. He likes old fullas.

Anyway, one of the nurses showed us where Tibby was and we go into her room and she's sittin in the garden wrapped up in a pink blanket. She was real tiny and skinny with grey hair and really black, smooth skin with no wrinkles I could make out. She had a real round face with big cheekbones and these big brown eyes and the longest eyelashes you ever saw. She was lookin right at me and reached out her tiny hand and took mine.

'I been waitin a long time for one of you mob to come through here,' she said in a real soft voice. 'By jeez, girl, you got that desert country look. Sit down with me. You aint in a hurry are ya?'

'No, Aunt,' I said, and introduced Antman just as the old fulla come round with Flea.

She looked at Flea, asked his name and called im over. He come straightaway. Like I said, he likes old fullas.

She picked up Flea and told us to take a load off and called for one of the nurses to bring us a cup of tea.

We got our tea and was makin a big racket stirrin the sugar in when we all looked at one other and busted out laughin.

'You fullas notice how whitefullas stir their tea real soft and us blackfullas make the biggest noise?' Aunt Tibby asked.

'Yeh.'

'When I was a kid,' she started, 'we used to have powdered milk cos you couldn't have the fresh stuff out our way and you had to stir it real hard so it dissolved without any lumps. Even later when we all got the fresh stuff we still did it. All you young fullas copied us and now it's a blackfulla thing. Don't matter how flash the blackfulla is, give im a spoon and cuppa and he's gunna make a racket.'

We reckoned she was right and started laughin again.

We sat there for a while waitin for Aunt to tell us what she wanted. It aint polite to pester old fullas. They tell ya when they're good and ready anyway.

She was nursin Flea, pettin im and tellin im what a

good lookin little fulla he was. He was lappin it up. Then she started to talk.

She told me that one of her mob had told her that they was talkin ta me and Ant down the pub the night before and when they found out my name and my country, they went straight up and told Aunty Tibby and she sent Lenny Boy to fetch us up to see her.

She asked me who my mob was and what part of Wongaibon country we come from and I told her.

She reckoned we was from the same tribe. Different families though. She said she aint been back to the red dirt country for a long, long time.

She started to cry and Ant passed her a tissue. She mopped up her tears and told us her story.

'I got married when I was real young. Only sixteen. Me husband was a whitefulla called Lenny. That's who young Lenny Boy's named after. He was a bit older than me, a drover. He was a good fulla. Real good to me and the kids. We had six of em. All good kids too. All of em live in other towns now. Got kids of their own. Young grandson Lenny lives here though, with his wife and their two kids. They look after me real good.

'Anyway, me and Lenny went drovin with the kids for years. All over the back country, Bourke, Tibooburra, Dubbo, all them places but we never went back to my country. Never. I used to beg him to take me home and he reckoned he would one day, but we never made it. We come here one time with a mob of cattle and Lenny got real sick and me and the kids had to finish the drive and come back here and settle and look after him. Somehow we never got back to my country. Me kids has never seen it and dunno what I'm goin on bout it for. Reckon this is where we call home. But it'll never be home to me. There aint no claypans for a start.

'Gawd we used to have some times with those old claypan dances. Your old grandmother Edie on the mouth organ, ya grandfather on the guitar, my old mother on the squeezebox. The ground was nice and smooth and ya didn't kick up too much dust. We'd have plenty of johnny cakes, and roo and emu. We'd make up cakes with the emu eggs for the kids. You aint never tasted anything better in ya life.

'I miss that red dirt. Specially the smell when rain or water fell on it. Even when Ma chucked the washin water over it. I crave that smell. And I miss the belah trees and the saltbush. And I miss the lingo. It's good hearin ya talk, girl, and lookin at that face. It's almost as good as bein home.'

I asked her how come she didn't go now and she reckoned the doctors wouldn't let her. It sure made me and Ant sad and Flea licked up a tear that fell on her soft old hand.

We yarned for a long time, told her about all the mob still livin out that way. She had a good laugh when I told her about Aunty Pearlie and Mrs G, and her eyes lit up when she heard bout Uncle Ronnie and how he got his sheep. She reckoned all the girls was mad on old Unc. I told her bout Ma and Dad and told her that a few of her mob still lived there. They was old but they sure would be glad to hear bout her. I told her everyone was always wonderin what happened to Old Lenny and Young Tibby. Last thing we told her bout was Cousin Moodle. Aunty Tibby reckoned Moodle was always mad on funerals. We could still hear her laughin when we walked outta the hospital later that night.

When we got back to the camp we made a big fire, had a feed and talked bout what we was gunna do for old Aunty Tibby.

The next mornin we got up early, packed up and drove all day to git back to my country. Everyone was real surprised to see us, but even more surprised when we told em about Aunt. They couldn't believe she was still alive. We all went down the Land Council and told em the story and they said they could organise a bus for those fullas who didn't have a motor car to go and see Aunty Tibby before she passed away.

You should have seen Aunt's face when the mob arrived at the hospital. Everyone camped for a couple of days and took turns goin to see her so we wouldn't tire her out too much. Lenny Boy reckoned he aint ever seen her that happy. He reckoned it was great to meet blackfullas with the same faces as him too.

She got real sad when we was leavin, but we all gave her photos and a biscuit tin full of red dirt from her country. We gave her saltbush and a branch from a belah tree. We may as well have given her a suitcase full of diamonds the way she carried on.

Aunty Tibby died not too long after. Lenny Boy reckoned she loved smellin the saltbush and was always pourin a little bit of water on the tin of dirt just so she could breathe in the smell.

Lenny Boy had a big blue with the rest of the family bout where she was gunna be buried. They reckoned her own country was too far away for em to visit her grave. They said he had no say. She was gunna be buried where she died.

Anyway, Lenny Boy got word to us and we all went to her funeral. One by one we all threw the red dirt, the saltbush and the leaves from the belah tree on her coffin. That night we played all the old songs in her memory. It rained the next day. We all hoped it would seep through the greyish-yellow clay and reach the red dirt so Aunty could smell it on her journey home.

Court day

Sometimes, when me, Antman and Fleabag are on the road, we call into one of the big towns on court day so we can catch up with Ant's cousin, Andrew, and his dog, Harry. Cousin Andrew is another one of Antman's lawyer cousins. Dunno what it is bout his mob, but they seem to turn out few of em. Got a coupla teachers and a copper as well.

Anyway, Andrew is a Koori Legal Aid lawyer, travels round the district courts representin all the blackfullas. He's been doin it for a while now. He always takes his beagle, Harry. You can tell if Andrew's doin a court, cos Harry sits out the front of the courthouse minglin with the mob. He's got a little rug and food and water bowls. All us blackfullas think Harry's just it. Harry don't hang with the town mutts cos they're always lookin for a blue and Harry is a lover, not a fighter. He gits on real well with Flea though.

Antman likes lookin on at the court. He reckons when we finish ramblin, he might go to uni and learn how to be a lawyer too. He's smart enough. Did real well at school.

Andrew used to be a hotshot lawyer in the city. He was married to a girl called Mai Britt from Sweden and they lived in a flash flat with harbour views. He was makin heaps of money and drivin flash cars and goin overseas all the time. Anyway, Mai Britt got homesick and they went to live in Sweden. This time Andrew got homesick. He pined for the rivers and the desert and the ocean and the sky of home. He reckoned the blue in Sweden was icy and pale, not deep and fiery like he remembered from home. He said there was no red in the earth and he was cold all the time.

He didn't understand the people, they laughed at different things. Even though he had Mai Britt, he was sick with loneliness. He just had to come home, but Mai Britt reckoned she was already home, so they parted.

When he got back, he went out home and got a job with the Aboriginal Legal Aid mob. One day he was travellin through a town and this old fulla was sittin out the front of the pub with a box with a puppy in it. It was Harry. Andrew took to im straightaway and the bloke reckoned he was lookin for a home for im. 'Purebred beagle,' said the old fulla. 'Got the papers to go with him too.'

He told Cousin Andrew he could have him for a carton of beer and smokes and Harry's been travellin round with Andrew, takin care of fullas in trouble with the law ever since. Andrew reckons he still misses Mai Britt, but he's happy cos he's at peace in his country and with his mob.

Anyway, this one time we see Harry out the front of the courthouse so we go over and Andrew's there talkin to clients. He's real happy to see us. So is Harry. He tells us to come in and watch the proceedings in court and we'll have a feed at lunch time. We leave Flea with Harry and go inside.

He gets a coupla offensive behaviours and drivin charges outta the way then he's got Choo Choo to deal with. Choo Choo's up on a possessin marijuana charge. He's a bit too fond of the old yahndi, is young Choo Choo. It's his first offence though and Andrew's got high hopes he'll be let off with a fine and a warnin, maybe some drug counsellin. Anyway, Andrew's goin on blah blah blah and handin the magistrate letters that say what a good fulla Choo Choo is and the old magistrate is readin em and he aint looked up from his bench so far.

When he finally does look up, there's Choo Choo standin there, all dolled up in his new court clothes and hat and lookin real shame. The old magistrate looks at im. 'Young man, you will show respect in my courtroom and remove your hat immediately.'

Choo Choo looks at the magistrate and says, 'I'm really sorry, Your Honour. I forgot I wuz wearin it.'

He reaches up and takes it off. When he does, the biggest bag a yahndi falls off his head and onto the ground in front of him. You could see the air rush outta Andrew. He shrivelled up to the size of a five year old.

Me and Ant along with a heap of fullas from the

public gallery had to rush outta the court so we could have a good laugh.

After a bit Andrew comes out, reckons we should just shut up bout Choo Choo for the moment and go and git a feed. He reckons we should go in his car. Trouble is, when we git to where it's supposed ta be parked, it aint there. We look down the road and see it goin real slow down the street. We run up after it and there's one of his offensive behaviours behind the wheel. He's drivin along as slow as an old slug on valium. We're walkin alongside, and Andrew leans in and says, 'Ya might wanna take the handbrake off, budda boy. That's if ya wanna git anywhere in a hurry.'

The fulla looks at Andrew and asks im what it's got to do with him.

Andrew tells im quick smart. 'It's my car you're driving, budda boy.'

The fulla stops and gits out. He's real shame, but that don't stop im from givin a mouthful a cheek ta Andrew.

'What stupid bastard puts the handbrake on out here?' he says. 'What do ya think it's gunna fuckin do? Roll away?'

He points down the long, flat road leadin outta town before he stomps away, his thongs kickin up a mini dust storm.

That afternoon, we decide to follow Andrew and Harry to the next town and chill out with a few beers and a feed. We're travellin real close behind him, when he stops to pick up a hitchhiker. We can't see him too clear cos of the dust from Andrew's car, but we see im git into the back seat. Harry always rides up front. Always!

When we pull up in town, the fulla gits out. He's the same one that tried to pinch cuz's car. He slams the door shut and walks off yellin, 'Thanks for the ride, cuzzo. See ya next time.'

Andrew gits out and comes over.

'Righto, you fullas. Let's git settled and git a few beers and a feed into us.'

We don't see nothin wrong with that suggestion.

Bringin the old ones home

Me, Antman and Fleabag was travellin through river country and decided to stop by and spend a coupla days with his cousin, Jake. Ant and Jake was real close, they grew up together and was more like brothers than cousins. It upset Jake a lot when Ant went to live in the city. He followed him for a while but couldn't settle. Said he couldn't feel his blackness in all that concrete. Couldn't see the stars, smell the earth or hear the whisper of the old fullas when it was quiet and dark.

Jake was real in touch with bein a blackfulla. He could read the earth and knew before any weatherman when it was gunna rain, when you was gunna have a drought, all that kind of thing. He knew when trouble and sad times was comin too, cos the willy wagtails told im.

Anyway, this time we pull up and there's no sign of Jake. The front door's open, but he always leaves it like that in case someone needs a feed or a bed and he aint home. So we walk outside and old Mrs McCormack calls out to us. We wander over. She'd know, if anyone would, what Jake was up ta.

She gives us a big kiss and picks up Fleabag for a cuddle and tells us that there's been some sorry business. Jake's been asked to take care of things. She doesn't want to go into anything cos she reckons it makes her feel funny inside, but says Jake'll tell us when we see im. 'He's down at the old waterhole,' she says, 'with a whole heap of other fullas.'

She tells us she's just seen Gus Hill walk past on his way to the pub with Jake's order. She reckons if we hurry we'd catch him and could fetch Gus and the supplies back out to Jake. It'd help everyone out.

Gus Hill is Jake's dog. A pure-white little fulla cept for a big tan heart on one side. He was wanderin past Jake's, lookin scrawny, tired, thirsty and hungry one day and Jake called im in. He give im a feed and a drink and told im he could hang around if he wanted to. Gus took im up on the offer. He had a tag round his neck with the name Gus Hill on it, but no one ever come lookin for im.

Anyway, Jake taught im how to do lots of things and Gus seemed happy to go along with it for his room and board. Cos Jake aint got a car or a phone, he puts messages in a little pouch round Gus's neck. He's taught him to go to the pub or store with his order and they bring Gus back with it later and collect the money. Sometimes if he's too pissed to walk, he'll send Gus round to relations or mates with messages if he needs to yarn with any of em.

Anyway, we decide to go and pick up Gus and go out and see Jake. We tell Mrs McCormack we'll catch up with her later and cruise off.

We git down the pub and there's Gus sittin inside with a bowl a water and a snack. He's real happy to see us and makes a bit of a fuss over his old mate, Fleabag. The publican, Curley, comes round from the counter to shake Ant's hand and give me a kiss. He shouts us a beer and we tell im we'll fetch Jake's order out for im.

We git out to the waterin hole and there's the biggest mob of fullas out there. Lots of kids and dogs, and lots of elders. Flea sees Jake and jumps outta the window and goes barrellin over to im. He looks real surprised to see him and grabs im and starts cuddlin im. We open the door and let Gus out and go over ta Jake. He starts cryin and grabs Ant and holds him real hard. Then he gits me in a bear hug.

'Whut the fuck you fullas doin ere?' he yells.

We tell im we was passin and thought we'd call by for a coupla days.

Ant asks im whut the sorry business was all about.

He tells us ta have a beer then we'd go for a walk.

Bout half an hour later we walk over to this mound and we sit on a log and he tells us the story.

'Some fulla out on one of the properties found a big heap of old bones lyin all together. He reported it to the police and they found out it was the bones of blackfullas who'd been shot round a hundred years ago. Anyway, the fulla felt real bad cos it woulda been his people whut done it. He went down to the Land Council and asked how he could set things right and they tell him he could have the bones reburied in the proper blackfulla way and if the old fullas whut died was happy, their spirits would come home to rest.

'So they come and asked me.

'I was real happy to do it. Those poor old ones' spirits would be out there floatin on the wind cos they died so violently. They must be buggered and need to rest in their own place by now.

'So I got together the mob and we collected the bones, and cleansed them in a smokin ceremony and wrapped them proper and reburied em and we had another smokin ceremony. Now we just waitin ta see if the old fullas are happy and comin home.'

Jake tells us to hang round if we want. We was real honoured to be asked and Jake took us to the burial place and we knelt beside the big mound and held hands while Jake sang a song in the lingo real quiet and soft. Gus Hill and Fleabag started to howl real soft too. It was scary and lovely at the same time.

That night we sat up eatin emu and johnny cakes and singin and yarnin. When ya went off into the scrub to go to the toilet you could hear the soft voices floatin on the wind. Later we all sat quiet. The whole place felt real peaceful. We could hear the river flow and the soft rustlin of the leaves on the big old trees. Jake reckoned the old ones would've sat under the same trees all those years ago. Then Jake told us all to not make a sound, so we went silent and suddenly we could hear the old fullas whisperin in the night. Jake reckoned they was happy and was on their way home.

Funny thing is, next morning we all woke up at the same time. We looked over and saw Flea, Gus and the rest of the dogs all lined up and lookin up into the sky. Their ears wuz all pricked. Next thing, we hear the biggest noise and look up and this big flock a cockatoos comes roarin over our heads and disappears into the sky.

Jake and everyone starts huggin one another and jumpin round. Jake comes over and grabs us both. 'They're home. The old fullas ave come home.'

We sure did celebrate that night. We invited the old farmer and his family along. Jake reckoned they really needed to know they done the right thing.

Acknowledgements

I would like to thank the following people: The nuns, in particular Sister Aquinas of St Mary's Convent, Hay; Jim Kable and the late Violet Medway, founder and former principal of Queenwood School for Girls: great teachers all who gave me a great education and belief in my abilities; Deb Armstrong, Debbie Barnier (nee Clarke) and Linda Keyte for being friends and supporters in the first difficult years in Sydney; Alan Randall, the late John Powlay and Mick Ford, who took me in and cared for me in one of my darkest hours; Mark Hogan, Sara Davidson and Gregory White, David and Christine Rollison and Christophe Lee, who gave me tremendous encouragement and support when I boldly said in 2004 that I was going to be a writer and have a book published.

Thanks also to Scott 'the big Queenslander' Dowie, who bankrolled my competition entries and shouted drinks when required; Terri McCormack, Gary Mitchell and Rebecca Jameson who lasered, printed and emailed for me and gave me friendship and encouragement; My mum, dad, brother, sisters, nieces, nephews, aunties, uncles and cousins and adopted sister, Shirley Lomas, for their unconditional love and for providing the inspiration for many of the stories that appear in this book; Irina Dunn whose support has meant a great deal to me; and my good mates from the Sir William Wallace Hotel who, through their fundraising efforts, ensured that I remained mobile and able to live my life.

I'd also like to thank the judges of the Unaipon Award for picking me as the winner in 2006; Janet Hutchinson for her invaluable suggestions; and Wendy Sanderson and UQP for making it all seem easy. Last, but certainly not least, I'd like to thank my good and enduring mate, Chris 'Erkus' Burke, who graciously allowed me to pilfer bits and pieces of his yarns and who has travelled with me, allowing me to see things and parts of the world I never would have thought possible.

FIRST NATIONS CLASSICS

Heat and Light by Ellen van Neerven
Introduction by Alison Whittaker

In this award-winning work of fiction, Ellen van Neerven leads readers on a journey that is mythical, mystical and still achingly real.

Over three parts, van Neerven takes traditional storytelling and gives it a unique, contemporary twist. In 'Heat', we meet several generations of the Kresinger family and the legacy left by the mysterious Pearl. In 'Water', a futuristic world is imagined and the fate of a people threatened. In 'Light', familial ties are challenged and characters are caught between a desire for freedom and a sense of belonging.

Heat and Light is an intriguing collection that heralded the arrival of a major new talent in Australian writing.

'A breathtaking work of art.' ***The Weekend Australian***

'A stunning debut from a young writer of immense potential.'
Melissa Lucashenko

ISBN 978 0 7022 6599 0

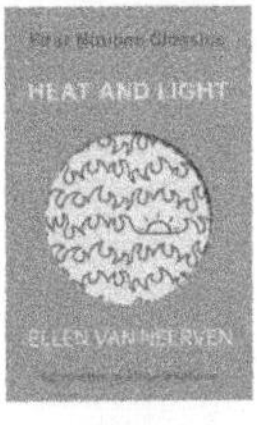